FLORA & JIM

FLORA & JIM

By BP Gregory

FLORA & JIM Copyright © 2018 BP Gregory

All Rights Reserved

ALL RIGHTS RESERVED. This work is copyright apart from any use permitted under the Copyright Act 1968. This work may not be reproduced or transmitted in part or in its entirety in any form or by any means, electronic or mechanical, including photocopying, recording, or by any information storage and retrieval system, nor may any other exclusive right be exercised, without the prior written consent of the author BP Gregory, except where permitted by law.

This is a work of fiction. Places and place names are either fictional, or used fictitiously. Any resemblance to persons either living or dead is purely co incidental.

ISBN-13: 978 0 6457319 2 7

Acknowledgments

Thank you to my amazing proof readers: Jason Steen, Ahren Morris, Diane Gregory, and Martin Gregory. Also to The Edible Bug Shop, for providing so much practical research (despite how they are portrayed in the novel, bugs can be quite tasty!).

Flora & Jim cover images by Lucie.K, JDW Tog Man, and Alexey U, Candy Foil interior image by Stock Design, The Town cover images by pavelr and Tim Bird, Orotund cover image by Alex Malikov, and Visit the House image by Peter Dedeurwaerder all courtesy of Shutterstock.

Content Advisory

This story features adult themes including animal violence, cannibalism, loss of a loved one, graphic violence/gore, mental health issues, and traumatic death. It may not be suitable for all readers.

Table of Contents

Copyright		v
Acknowledgments		vii
Content Advisory		ix
Chapter One	Pursuit	1
Chapter Two	Harvest	21
Chapter Three	Sweet Home	41
Chapter Four	Migration	69
Chapter Five	Postcards from Fauna	89
Chapter Six	The Moss Trap	115
Chapter Seven	Gourmet	135
Chapter Eight	Glacier	149
Also by BP Gregory		165

FLORA & JIM

Chapter One

Pursuit

It wasn't immediately clear what had happened. Otherwise, I like to think I might have reacted better.

But my exhilaration, squinting through the slits of crude snow goggles, zeroed in on those tantalizing figures racing ahead. The other father and his young son. Biggie and shorty, just like little Flora and me. They were paper cut-outs against the light, where a collapse had conspired to open up buildings and let them through.

The crisp air that whooshed the skyscraper canyon could be a dirty old liar; it bit your face so bad, made eyes water; but they looked so close! Like I could stretch just a little more and close mittened fists around them. Imagine rummaging in those bags!

If their desperate flight made any sound it was obliterated by the harsh chug of my own pipes. Adrenaline crackled in delirious conduit from the other father to me, along the icy tarmac.

—*fear*—

My heart swelled. Picked up lead feet eagerly. Fear was the path I'd tread to finally, finally catch them.

No.

—*wait*—

Torturous breathing spluttered. The kid had stopped!

Abandoning all sanity shorty was turning back toward me. His guardian pawed frantically at his arm.

Inexplicable, I know, but I slowed. They weren't playing the game that made it ok to chase. Silhouetted by afternoon glare the son especially was becoming harder to see the nearer I trudged. The light fractured into whirling colours.

My forsaken youth had been filthy with similar signs and wonders, at least to my callow eyes. To see one pop up here was like falling into some dizzy hallucination.

Picture books I'd obsessed over of the old sun burning through Madonna blue, hellfire crimson poured on the floor: the stained glass of cathedrals that no longer existed. Bright-bleeding saints, who'd frown down on you shivering in your pew. Damning illumination with nowhere to cower and hide.

A frail replica made of candy wrappers around a candle stub

had resisted the slithering darkness by my childhood bedside. Like it was ever going to win.

All this rushed back as, stern as any martyr with the light boiling past, the boy pointed.

—pointing at me??—

Irresistibly I quailed. Victim of the bad child that huddled in the brainstem, forever in guilt at being uncovered. The weird dissociate conviction lingered that this was indeed a game, not life or death. Played by innocents, all. And I'd somehow missed the rules.

The other father was becoming hysterical.

—behind—

His son was pointing behind me.

—had to be some kind of trick—

I looked anyhow. Even though the cumbersome goggles meant swinging all the way around. Shorty's imperious finger demanded it.

To turn at the boy's urging and see Flora meters back, when she ought to have been treading on my heels. In the heat of the chase flat out in the middle of the road, like a toddler having a tantrum …

I all but screamed at my baby girl, the most treasured thing in what passed for my life.

'Fuck's sake, Flora, GET UP!'

Infuriated, I ripped the goggles off; their weight had been bowing my scarecrow neck. The world flipped too quick from narrow safe letterbox to a cold sea of light. A deluge. We were way beyond self-control, here. The boy had tickled my paranoia, and I'd had a gutful of being scared. I wanted to smash fear's spine with my boot.

'*FLORA*! Fuck, look, they're getting away! Would you

come on!'

Taking advantage, the other father bundled his child up to run. Feet drummed the pavement and they dissolved into the glare. Going, going. Gone.

'FUCK!'

My impotent frustration clanged off rotten vacant buildings, this rotten empty city. Too loud to be taken back. Foolishly like some hothead teen I stood clenching and unclenching my fists as the echo rang out.

Embarrassing. But we'd been so close!

—come on, jimbo. for chrissake, get a hold of yourself—

—don't scare your girl—

Silence crept slyly back in to drape the street. Only the lying wind lingered, whistling in blank windows to remind us how tiny we were. And Flora was not getting up.

Without the chase-fever to inflame me, sanity came as a chill slap to the head. Too late, my fuming squint picked the key detail across the distance. The sickening way Flora's small limbs were hammering the tarmac, the gnawing air, her brittle self, as though to drum all these from reality.

My miserable gut shivered inside-out.

Already slipping and skittering back to where my daughter fluttered, like a bird cast down.

—fuck's sake, flora, get up!—

Have you ever, there in the moment, regretted something so hard you'd wipe the universe clean to undo it?

All I can say is, lucky such extravagant power rarely gets granted. Otherwise we'd be doomed anew every time a worm like me stepped in his consequences.

—not so fast, jimbo—

Wanting only to go faster. The sled jerked and skidded behind my measured lunges.

—steady, steady—

I just wanted to reach my baby girl.

It was the same issue that made pursuit of the other father so hellish: we couldn't afford to sweat. Perspiration would chill inside our snug clothes the moment we paused for a breather, and that would be it, goner, thanks for playing.

Flora's seizure was easing even as I reached her. Sick with remorse and all, I still couldn't help myself. On my knees by my ailing daughter still I glanced hopefully up, searching for a last glimpse of the other father.

Already it was like they'd never existed.

Other people often seemed ghostly concepts, hard to believe in, but these two I could never let go. They had come along at precisely the wrong time with their smiles and bulging backpacks. If it be with my last breath, I was going to hunt the other father down and take what was his. For Flora.

Nothing but stark light filled the street. Reluctantly, I turned my attention to making my baby safe. Tremors drained out like water. Her thin limbs settled slowly in their bulky padding. It had been exactly "nine-avocado" from when I noticed she was down. A slow nightmarish count, performed automatically.

—when the damn boy pointed her out, the boy!—

So I guess you could say Flora's latest bout of rattling stopped quickly. It never felt quick. Only like the most horrible helpless forever.

Mai had claimed fits might be a childhood phase. Mai, my wife, wise Mai had hoped they might get shorter, and eventually fade away as Flora grew up. Counting had been our prayer.

She had an epic accumulation of study on what could go wrong with babies. With a child on the way, one of us had to be obsessed. One of us had to know.

Flora's birth still haunted my thin dreams. Mai spouting a clenched-tooth litany of natal disaster, interrupted only by shrieking for her own life. She called out against rupture, infection, and shock. While I stood ineffectually by. Not even knowing the correct way to be terrified.

Now it was down to me, I was the only one. What could kill Flora? I liked to beat my chest and claim nothing, so long as I stood by her side. Everything. Let's say, a sniffle, or a rotten tooth. I'd been mourning from the moment she was born. Even with my limited experience I don't know how Mai was able to carry all this in her head and live.

I clumsily wrung mittened hands, and in a spasm of loathing hurled away the chunk of rubble Flora had slipped on. Probably struggling to keep up with her Daddy, who'd charged heedlessly on like some asshole who didn't deserve kids.

Weeping russet rebar jutted from the concrete hereabouts. It jabbed in all directions, like broken fingers. Without the thick unravelling crown of her mother's balaclava Flora's conk on the nonce might have been fatal.

Good solid plans run through stiffening fingers real quick in the cold. Only ever nine-avocado away from disaster. Look at me, shuffling around ruins chanting nonsense to a mythical fruit.

When I was a kid, the Family (not *my* little family, the one I chose and built; rather, the elderly collective who raised me) used to claim that survivors simply *wanted* life more.

'Dying's not so bad, Jimmy,' they'd tried to explain.

Because, hell, that's what a growing lad wants to hear from his so-called caregivers.

'You just lie yourself down, and decide that's as far as you go. Anyone can manage it. Besides, we'll all be getting there eventually.'

I wasn't a bright kid, but deep down even I knew that here was a conceit that couldn't ring true. Look at the sprawling city, the suburbs, the world beyond. We loved life harder than all those people?

Some Family members hadn't even *liked* life. They cursed it, and their own infirmities, with a passion. Filled every day with loathing. Uncle Isaiah, I'm looking at you, you sour old bastard.

If I had to come up with a theory, if only to fly in the face of my elders, I reckoned ongoing life was by accident. A series of modest, critical strokes of fortune that others missed out on. And that was why snow filled *their* mouths, while Flora and I struggled on. Not entirely sure who was luckier.

I yanked the sled alongside, and began making room for my girl. It wasn't a proper sled; just some sturdy toddler bath I scrounged, but by some quirk its scratched pink plastic held firm in the outside cold instead of shattering into brittle splinters. Bound to go eventually, though. Everything broke, and there was no replacement.

—*the last of our kind, every one*—

Being for luxuries, the sled often skittered along empty. We weren't silly. Survival items were kept protected under clothes, where they'd have to be stripped from our corpses to be taken.

Body heat bound up by cloth made a frail bubble. Rapidly dwindling as I knelt in the street. Ice stabbed up through my kneecaps, every gust of breeze a cheese grater. As soon as you step outside you're on the clock.

Picture a glimmer at your core. A spark, tiny and frail. Outside exposure rummages for that spark with blunt merciless fingers. Digging deep, freezing tissue black as it goes. And if it ends up touching that spark, well, you'll go out.

Ok. Sled ready.

Even mummified in all her layers it was nothing, no effort, to lift Flora in. Like with a touch more carelessness it would be possible to fling her right into the sky.

She wasn't growing, and I shuddered, stuffing both mittens over my mouth to contain a vast helplessness that'd do neither of us any good. This aghast trembling, these tears freezing into scratchy wool one hundred percent did not matter. Work needed doing. I was not having the alternative for my daughter.

Being haggard created too many seams, and my face had sprung a leak. I couldn't remember crying so much in my youth. I'd been surrounded by too many quick to tell me what a man was; handing down the guff imposed on them like it was a sacred trust. Now, so long as Flora didn't catch me at it, I could bleed off the pressure as often as I wanted. Healthier, and to hell with Aunt Abena and the rest. I'd be my own man.

I tucked my girl in tight, wanting all fingers and toes accounted for. Little bird into her nest. And then reluctantly turned into whatever tracks we'd made.

Wasn't much. The occasional boot print for the sled to bump over. Retreating when situations went awry was one of our rules. Never make new plans on the march. It's too cold to think straight.

Buckets of such rules, we had. Flora could sing the lot of them upside down and inside out, my good girl. Blissfully oblivious to the whole cloth I cut from.

Reversals aside, we needed to recover and keep pushing forward. This vast metropolis, once stuffed to the gills, could scarce support one man and a sparrow of a girl.

'*What about us?*' I wanted to howl at those who built it, those teeming masses now blameless in their graves. '*What were you going to leave for our future?'*

Electric lights still sparkled in the memory of the Family's oldest surviving member. Aunt Amelia was probably more accurately Great-Great-Grandma Amelia, but all the ladies of the Family had been Aunts to me, all the gentlemen and not-gentlemen Uncles.

As a lad I'd seen piped water for myself, running from a tap instead of bubbling ice in a pot. The tank snugged in steaming faecal pits to keep it from bursting. These were modest past wonders I tried to keep alive for Flora in stories.

Heading back to our last camp cast a shadow on our heart for another, more urgent reason. There was always the chance Mai might catch up if we didn't step along right quick. I didn't have the fortitude left in me for that. Not today.

When the scuffling footprints we followed degraded into a drunken waltz, I knew we were close. *Don't leave a trail to your door* was another of our rules that sounded good, and may or may not help.

Outward bound this morning I'd made a game of it. A little dance to make Flora giggle. Her laugh was a cracked wheeze and she peeked through mittens as though she didn't mean to, which made me cherish it all the more.

My anxiety eased at the sight of tumbled bluestone. Yes, this was it. Some of the heavy blocks appeared to have mysteriously erupted and slithered downhill, but I knew it was frost that did that. Squeezed them from the soil like pips. The cellar door still gaped welcomingly. Best guess, this had been a gentrified pub.

Even now, many buildings kept their secrets. Aunt Amelia claimed we'd the last round of "haves" to thank for that. Back when there'd been such an archaic concept as wealth. Everything ended, and the haves hadn't been able to resist their nature. In a last gesture of meanness they locked everything tight.

Society devolved rapidly, after, Amelia recounted with relish. More like how things had always been underneath. And nobody had to pretend anymore.

Luckily for Flora and me tonight, carousing had been an artefact of the early days. Generations drank themselves dry and succumbed, having lost their sense to come in out of the cold. Nobody had seen the value in securing an empty cellar.

I carefully lifted my daughter down, sled and all. Murmuring, 'Easy, honey,' in case she felt the change as a frightening jolt. No idea what penetrated the twilight following a seizure, but a loving voice couldn't hurt. And if in no other way useful, it eased my own twisting powerlessness, an ache rivalling my weary arms and legs.

Next step was to get the air heated up a bit. Down here we were mercifully out of the wind which *felt* warmer. The comfort was deceptive; well below par to sustain life. Sit your creaky ass down to rest in a corner of the dark, draughty space, oh only for a second, and that would be where your statue rested forever.

Of course, the two of us couldn't heat the whole cellar to liveable. Cramped as it was, that would be extravagance beyond my dreams.

I got to work stringing layered tarps over twisted coat hangers to make us a cosy pocket. Two sheets for a crude airlock, and I made sure the cute duck-print sheet was inner for Flora to see when she woke.

Fire was a challenge. Modernity left little that was safe to burn, especially around high density housing. In Amelia's tales folk smashed and kindled their glue-filled furnishings anyhow, not seeing a lot of choice between slow extinction or quick.

For years the sky had glowered brown, closer than it should be. Great pillars of smog climbing against the clouds. When snow stuttered down it came clogged and grey. The last great tribute to the vanished epochs of industry.

That's when Aunt Amelia would laugh, because obviously the end result was that the glaciers came in so much faster. No disaster too great for humanity to find a way to fuck themselves harder.

My stories didn't always come from others. I'd been living a life of my own. Once, I found a stick. Made of actual wood.

Just lying behind some rubble like it had sprung up out of the ground, which as I understand it once upon a time had been the most natural thing in the world. Plants did that. I've seen diagrams. But this stick was out of its time, worlds away from any explanation.

I picked it up, expecting the hallucination to vanish. How smooth and light it seemed! How natural it felt in my hand. An organic shape, which had come about by reaching longingly for a sun that had been different, in ways I couldn't quite grasp.

Warmer, Aunt Amelia insisted. Comforting like a good fire. Golden pure kindness flooding your skin, and you didn't need to hide your eyes in fear of frying your retina. Inevitably she cried, making it not quite believable.

Now I finally got it. That stick was heartbreaking to hold. Relic of a whole branch of life snapped off the cooling planet. There were no trees anymore. No crops. No grass, so far as anyone had seen.

I carried it reverently for as long as I could. Which amounted to two whole days before I had to burn it.

Flora and I burned oil, mostly. In a shallow tinfoil dish with a strip of rotten cloth for a wick. Flora called the stuff "mush" because of the way it solidified at ambient temperature (cold) into a sort of lumpy puke-coloured wax. One lamp might not seem much, but if your space was modest it did the job.

Occasions where we had anything to cook were celebrated by firing up dried patties of our carefully saved poo to make the fire, mixed with upholstery or whatever was on offer. Much warmer. And once desiccated and crumbly it didn't reek too bad.

Not that we were reckless. Fearful of disease, we wore ancient non-biodegradable bags over our hands for handling the fresh product. Cloth face-caps later to avoid breathing the smoke.

With the sheltering tarps giving the occasional flap and rattle it was just the little lamp today, quicker to get going. With two fingers I scooped some gluey mush onto the wick and got the party started.

Once we had light, the blue plastic walls took on a friendly glow. 'Our pond,' I often called it to Flora, and waved the duck sheet like they were swimming.

We laid out our pond the same way each time. The lamp balanced in a corner where we were unlikely to kick it even in restless sleep. Assuming we didn't go up in flames, it'd be an unforgivable waste of mush.

I waited until it was warmer—never truly warm, but warm *enough*—and then gently examined my sleeping daughter. She was unlikely to remain under much longer. My own fingers, nose and ears were crinkling into painful life at the shift in temperature.

As I'd suspected, my poor girl had wet herself during her fit. I didn't fancy the intense neon shade of that urine, either. She needed to be drinking more water. Thankfully the removable cloth pads sewn into her pants had soaked up the worst of it.

I took them out, and wiped the rest of the bright wee from her bony shanks before it could burn. Not so different to changing her as a baby; although now if the rash became too angry she'd be unable to walk, and we'd lose the other father's trail completely.

I was quite pleased with inventing the pads in Flora's pants, it was satisfying to see them work. Years of necessity had made me quite the sewing dilettante, Frankenstitching "servicables" from scavenged rags and sleeping bags. Clothing was vital. I dreaded the day the seams might let go.

Tucked into the sled was our disintegrating defensive gear, originally motorcycle armour, which I used for exploring new neighbourhoods. I'd taken it from a stricken man, long ago. I was less cautious in those days. Less desperate, too, although it hadn't felt like it.

I came upon the unlucky fellow lying in the middle of an intersection with a broken back. Looked for all the world as though he'd been thrown there in a motorcycle accident. Never mind that there was no traffic, no vehicles. Both vanished artefacts of old Aunt Amelia's childhood.

I scratched my scalp through my balaclava and stared at the puzzle of the time travelling motorcyclist. First from a distance. Then up close.

As I circled and chewed my lip I was nothing but an impertinent disruption to a man's sacred final hours. He wouldn't talk to me. I wouldn't either, were I in his position. His visor was half up and he stared at the clouds with glazed eyes, trying to go away, in the only manner left him. Wearing silence that would carry him off.

It only occurred sometime later that he must have been all armoured up to confront some animal. Superstitious chills. Thank heaven nosy impetuous men never ran afoul of it.

Took me a while, but I yelped in triumph when I finally deduced he'd plummeted from a building. Helmet flinched a bit at the noise. Pleased with my sleuthing and curious enough to make the effort, I laboured up fourteen flights and found the broken window.

At this height the wind roared, sucking from outside, wouldn't mind a taste of me for afters. Keeping a determined hold on the frame I peered down, confirming trajectories. But for the life of me I couldn't work out what anyone would have been up here for.

The building only offered empty offices, the most numerous and useless breed of real estate. Cold steel and crazed glass. Carpet tiles pulled up. Not even any paper. There had to have been a reason.

Disgruntled, I returned to the street and crouched over the motorcyclist, all splayed out.

There was enough wherewithal in those bloodshot eyes to follow me. My noise had upset him. He was breathing in anxious huffs that fogged the visor, making him blink rapidly. His nose was grey. Lips violet. No telling how long he'd lain there trying to die.

I was about to upset him more. The injury paralysed movement, but not feeling. As I unzipped the man's jacket and began manipulating stiff limbs to take it off he screamed. High. Unrelenting. In incandescent agony.

I almost took my hands off him, but remembered my family and stuck my chin out. The family I chose, the one with the small "f". We needed these things more than him.

Still, I was glad nobody could see. It was shameful that a human being couldn't be left to die in peace. There was only indignity heaped on pain, right to the bitter end.

It's one thing to grit your teeth, see, and say, 'I'm doing this for others. It's the right thing.' But your heart calculates all the ways you benefit, and it knows a vile act. It twists from it. Never forgets.

He screamed the whole time and by the end there wasn't much voice left in that convulsing throat. His ruddy beard jutted like something electrified. Tears rolled freely down the sides of his head and froze his long hair to the ground.

I wept, too. It wouldn't be the same good man returning to my wife and child tonight.

I left the motorcyclist naked. A sallow broken starfish with only a rasp of a voice, staring up at the sky. Guess the only mercy was he wasn't shivering. He couldn't have much longer to wait.

Our clothing would hold another day. I wrapped my Flora up to hug some heat into her. My baby. Let me be the monster, if only she gets to live. I'll do anything to keep her safe.

'Daddy?'

Flora began stirring, groggy. Doubtless her noggin ached like nobody's business. I gently rolled the oversize balaclava off to expose her pinched features. Showing your face was what you did to connect with people, to reassure them: I'm human, you're human. All humans in this together.

It was pretty common for skin that regularly braved the outside to not have much feeling or expression. Members of the Family had suffered from *rigor facia*, shambling about with clay masks over the tender meaty core that had to be presumed still in there.

Flora had it worse than anyone I'd ever seen. Unwrapped, her blank dolly face stared up at me. I'd become accustomed to reading even the slightest twitch.

'Right here, baby.'

I raised my own balaclava.

'I gotcha. You had an oopsie.'

'Sorry. Daddy, I'm sorry.'

She was near tears; that twisted the knife.

'I didn't have the traffic cone smell.'

Mai reckoned some people smell oranges before a seizure but we'd only seen pictures, a type of fruit. How the hell was Flora supposed to know what an orange was? Eventually we got the concept tangentially across by colour, hence "traffic cone smell". I didn't mind the traffic cone.

Other times right before she went stiff Flora's eyes would widen, staring into eternity, and she'd whisper the sky was coming down to bite her. Save me Daddy. Which creeped me out so bad I didn't want to be near her. It was easier to be brave when Mai was still around.

I hugged my daughter harder, if that was possible, pressed her blank face into my shoulder.

'Never mind, sweetie.'

I so very much wanted to groan, 'Daddy's sorry he was so mean,' but my tongue was a slab of rock. She relied on me to be perfect.

'Sleepy,' Flora mumbled against my coat. Being a child she was happy to cuddle with me forever. Wrapped in the body heat of two where she would safely, warmly starve.

For me, it was like cradling a bundle of frail twigs. Flora was too small to make much difference to my comfort. At night my feet never truly defrosted and I was leery of accidentally crushing her.

I missed Mai's generous arms more than anything. It was the only time I can remember being truly and completely toasty, and to think I'd once had that for free, on tap, every night. Just seemed outrageous now. I guess everybody longs for that one embrace whole enough to keep the world out.

'Sh, that's ok baby. No sads. You tuck your head down and have a nap. Daddy's popping out for a bit.'

'Nooo …'

Clutching my sleeve, already slipping under. Life was a constant state of anxiety knowing that anyone around you could evaporate, no notice, gone. And these episodes left her exhausted, sparse muscles a greenish bruised mess.

'I don't want you to go, Daddy, *please*. I'll be good.'

I kissed my daughter's forehead.

'You're always my good girl. I'll only be gone a mo.'

Like promises meant any more than the breath they travelled on. Flora held fast anyhow, carrying it down with her into sleep.

Back outside the wind was beginning to hiss. Light already waning, and the sky a low cottony blanket. Sullen, not too angry. You had to read the clouds, they had tips concerning your very immediate future. I took the risk and went kicking through the city's lengthening shadows for snow.

Wind brings snow in at night as an afterthought, when it squeals across the frozen sky to push weaker buildings over. Huddled in our pond we've listened fearfully to the roar, the heavens crashing down. The floor shakes. Maybe some bricks drop from your own ceiling and you know nowhere's safe.

Well. I do. I whisper to Flora, 'It's a long way off, baby. Go back to sleep.' And if I can stare raw-eyed into the night until dawn, my will will ward it off happening to us.

Rare to see flakes falling. The weather's generally too dry or too cold here, I forget which. But little drifts collect in corners so it must be snowing somewhere.

I hit the jackpot down an alley, hiding from the sun. We never drink snow, given the choice. Often it glitters with funny colours in the light, unwholesome crystals I can't explain. I worry that having floated in the sky it's more contaminated. All fears and no answers, me. We prefer to strain frost from chunks of topsoil for drinking.

Kneeling, I squeezed handfuls of snow to help it melt and scrubbed the absorbent pads. Absently one ear was aware I had to hurry—the wind was really starting to croon. Whipping around sharp corners it sounded like voices sometimes, like the city was still alive, which was a joke.

Night was on its way. And while the distant sun offered little comfort, it would be suicide to venture out without. I was caught between imperatives to hurry, but a job rushed is a job half-done.

Tucking the cleaned pads away for re-use, I retrieved a small bottle kept safe in an inner pocket. Thick brown glass, like old medicine. Didn't want this one breaking. From it I carefully sprinkled a few drops of my own cloudy urine over the discards of the crude laundry.

Couldn't have some animal getting it in their snoot that there was an unguarded child about. Assuming my thin piss'd suffice to scare them off. I tried to feel big and scary when making it, at least, practiced some self-conscious war cries.

The real world hadn't turned out much like I imagined when I was a kid, safe in my library and obsessed with hunting animals. Used to dream how everyone'd be so proud of me when I finally dragged one home, clap me on the back, etcetera. Because of course I'd be better than the Family's scouts who'd been doing this all their lives. I was me.

The tension, I thought, was the lateness of the day. My sour memories and eagerness to return to Flora. Even sheltered in the alley, the wind came past my face so fast now it gave a horrible drowning sensation.

Wasn't until I tried to about-face and go back to my girl, and found myself unable to twitch a muscle, that I realised who stood in the mouth of the alley behind me. Staring with her unkind eyes.

Have you ever been so afraid you felt welded in place? My body was on lockdown, hoping not to be noticed. Dark down here. The shadow of the buildings dropped over the alley. She might have come sniffing around like a beast. Drawn by two urines mingled, the scent of the family she missed.

And to think once upon a time my most fervent wish was for my wife to never leave me. I would crave her so hard blood sprang from my gums. When I kissed her it stained her lips crimson like some woman in a magazine, only a hundred times more beautiful; I told her so every morning the moment I opened my eyes. She'd groan and mock-swat me as I covered her face in red kisses, and we made our own heaven.

—*don't move*—

What did she want now? Bloodier kisses, no doubt.

—*jim!*—

My ears strained over the crackling wind, breathless for any hint that could tip the moment one way or another. Could she see me? I remained still, and the sun crept down the sky. A tiny bleeding point, searing without heat. Lighting up the clouds.

Through a traitorous dusty pane a finger of gold stabbed into the alley where I stood motionless, staring at the wall.

—*here he is, here!*—

It singled me out in slivers, isolated slices of Jim floating in the dimness. My shirt had ridden down too far and I could feel blisters forming on the back of my neck at that touch. The risk of sweat.

—*jim! some …*—

She wasn't going to let me leave. Scrabbling panic. Tears and snot froze the lower part of my balaclava, dragging it down, blocking what air I could pull in. When peeled from my face later it would take beard and skin as a souvenir.

This was where I stood, frozen. The other father always ahead, unable to be caught. My wife behind, and I could not escape. I imagined Flora whimpering and calling for me as the lamp went out. She'd die waiting in that cellar.

'Mai, go away,' I gagged. 'Stop following me.'

—flora—

It was for her that I found the strength to swing around, my eyes screwed shut and balls the size of raisins.

I barked, 'You can't have her!'

Sun on my face. A cackle from the wind. No assault, though, nothing jumped me.

Fearfully I cracked one eye open. Sprang them both.

Nobody was there.

FLORA & JIM

Chapter Two

Harvest

Prey to the first nibbling of panic I squeezed the cosmetics tube til my wrists cramped. Clumsily rolled and unrolled the damn thing, as though that might help.

The tube was like doll furniture between my massive cold-stiffened digits. Breath plumed from my mouth in clouds, obscuring the matter, and all the while Flora looked up at me imploringly with her big eyes.

I must've poked the last of the soothing jelly up my own

snout that morning without realising. Now even those final dabs were gone. Couldn't scrape any out of my moustache, which bristled from my face like spider's legs emerging from a cave.

Stalling, unable to meet her eyes I examined the list of ingredients, sounding out the tiny script. Aloe? If it was a plant it was extinct, along with the rest.

Feeling sick I showed Flora the flattened tube.

'Sorry, sweetheart. There's no more. We're just going to have to be brave.'

Flora mutely rolled her balaclava back down. Still, I caught the maroon crusting both nostrils, the tears glimmering above, and I felt like a monster. My little girl was crying because the dry air shredded nasal membranes and I didn't have any more ointment to put up her nose.

Familiar anxiety rolled my hands into fists. More than anything I longed to drop the tube and flee. Just blunder off blindly through the icy maze of streets until I didn't have to be me anymore. Who in their right mind would hand me a child?

—seriously, get your shit together, jim. you're the grownup—

Easier when Flora wore that sagging wool second face over her own, studded with lumps and waving threads. What colour had it been originally? Unassuming grey, now. The coward's urge passed. I was Daddy again.

I knelt to rub her knobbly spine, aware at that proximity how gamey we both smelled, and gestured ahead to our frozen shelter for the night. Still a ways off, but we were getting there.

'See this, honey, this one here? Look at all the balconies. It'll be grasshoppers for sure. I'll just bet.'

Impossible to know just by looking at four walls what lurked dormant inside; but pretending staved off tears and made my daughter smile instead. For that shy, almost imperceptible quirk of the eyes I'd slap a tin on my head and dance until the sky came down to bite us both.

'Maybe we'll find another goat, Daddy?'

I recoiled as though Flora had branded me.

'The goats are all fucking gone!'

Lashed out from that raw hollow place before I could help myself. And realised too late that Flora was trying to be funny.

These were the things my daughter said to jolly me out of a snit. She shouldn't have to. For the thousandth time I resolved to pull my socks up and be a better fucking father. It shouldn't be this hard.

Who could blame her for clinging to the memory of the goat? It wasn't a true recollection for Flora, not really. She'd been too young to retain much beyond atavistic warmth and the anomaly of a full belly. Cramped us both up good, which likely had no part in rosy remembrance. But after we'd crawled, weeping, wasteful, from our respective puddles of sick there'd been still more to stuff the emptiness.

I for one couldn't find it in my heart to condemn her. Especially not when it'd spark such questions as, 'Why are you sad, Daddy?' Instead, to gloss over my outburst I straightened with a groan and resumed trudging.

A long, pensive pause I thought would never end. True purgatory. Then finally I heard Flora following.

That put me back to trying to stow my second and third thoughts about this location. Chivvying Flora along aside, I hadn't loved it while scouting yesterday and even less today. Sadly we weren't exactly drowning in alternatives.

Progress went in slow two-step "hops". I donned our crumbling armour to spend day one locating our next appropriate castle, while Flora waited snug at the last. Come home, prepare overnight, and we'd both move the next day.

Rinse and repeat. With half a brain in your head you'd never dream of exposing your child until you knew the next nook to be safe when night fell. I assumed everyone else travelled in such short bursts. Hadn't exactly had an opportunity to ask.

It seemed the other father and his dumpling of a kid weren't getting appreciably far ahead, so that was something. Already that day when Flora hit her head seemed a fairy tale, like it had happened to some other daughter. We had journeyed through most of the city proper since then without ever again coming so close.

My true measure of passing time was Flora and I gnawed my cheek bloody that she seemed no bigger. Spindly sticks all tied with wool. Would she ever reach higher than my elbow? For that matter, what age did a woman menstruate? Oh God— where would I get a bra? I couldn't sew *that* well.

All terrifying, but my worst fear was that these little crises might never pop up. That she was too broken, damaged by my inability to provide.

—*we aren't goners yet*—

And we'd stay that way so long as we stuck to the routine. Could be a shorter or longer routine, depending on the distance to next shelter, but it was still the routine.

I particularly didn't enjoy how much of this district looked industrial. We'd grown used to the safe colourlessness of other parts of the city: grey, grey. All curling in genteel resignation to the ground. It fit the portrait the Family had always painted of what was out there.

Here, the massive walls wept red, passionate Mai's favourite colour. The unlovely buildings were clogged with vast rusting tangles of arcane machinery. Titans of manufacture, dwarfing the structures they had inhabited.

When the contested flow of oil and electricity stopped, looked like they had died in the process of clawing free to search for more. The looming corpses still bled with the slow advance of frozen water. If you could restore the juice and flick a switch, would they twitch? Reach for you?

'It'd be very bad luck to go poking around inside,' I cautioned Flora, wagging a solemn finger in her woolly face. 'No matter how curious you get. The machines' angry ghosts are still trapped in those buildings. The walls were built to keep them there.

'And if they lay hands on you they might gnaw the insides out of your bones, or burn you red as their rust, or steal hair and teeth away while you sleep, for making their nests with.'

Such was the best language I had for describing the radiation hazard. It seemed to make an impression. And it really did feel like hostile spirits were watching avidly from within their cinderblock prisons. Helped my fib along enormously, and made me wish I'd kept my trap shut.

Both today and yesterday were overcast, weather I dreaded trudging through because of the way indistinct nooks became bottomless pits. Anything could be poised to leap out from anywhere.

During reconnaissance the asshole wind had kicked trash about enough to have me convinced I'd heard something, twisting about. Now my back felt properly fucked. Small mercies Flora hadn't been there to witness my performance.

I hadn't even been able to be sneaky. Had to parade right down the middle of main street in front of God and whoever, as the only way to avoid the snakes of leprous rust that colonised the sidewalk. The ghosts, stretching long tendrils from beneath collapsed doorways. Oh boy did I wish I hadn't told that tale.

—*step on a crack and you'll break your father's back*—

The breeze tittered. If not for the subtle hints the other father had been this way I'd have sprinted out of dodge, for sure, and never looked back. By the time I stumbled on the closest we'd get to a refuge, my feet were blistered and nerves chewed to threads.

Didn't love it, but I liked leaving Flora alone for so long even less. Strained imagination offered up Mai, curved longingly over our daughter in my absence. Stealthily lifting a corner of the crusted blanket to press across our baby's sweet sleeping face.

Stop it, Jim. It was all this red that had her on my mind.

The rest of the seeping district drew back from this one small block, which was what caught my eye. The lack of rust made it the most wholesome option I'd seen. In odd isolation a circle of apartment buildings had once loomed about a flat tarmac pool, with tubular play equipment jammed in the middle.

Not enough remained to determine if the isolated circle had been some unprofitable concern banished to the boonies, or low income housing. Cities needed underpaid manpower to wipe their asses but they didn't like to look at it. Shoddy housing often cropped up in these undesirable neighbourhoods.

Only one of the set of buildings remained standing, now. Around the circle the others had shielded this last lonely sibling as they were gnawed to their foundations by the weather. Bereft of their protection wouldn't be long before it followed suit. Just adequate to sling a roof over our heads for the two nights we needed to move on.

Back when all the buildings had been in place their pitted faces had been arranged inward. It couldn't have been an accident that every balcony leered down at the play equipment, pinned in the middle. As we passed with the sled scraping along I was relieved Flora showed no inclination to scale its crumbling remains.

But then, why would she? She had no idea children were supposed to run and play. Let alone there'd once been specialised equipment for it.

Mai and I failed to lift a single precious book, children's or otherwise, from the Family's extensive library. 'Where was the need?' we claimed smugly. We planned on holding our child's tiny hand and telling her everything she needed to know. The adoring voices of her parents in a continuous narration of the world as seen through our loving eyes.

It was to be the opposite of the Family's bleak, dead-end philosophy. And I let it happen because I thought I'd grown up in the *real world*. I was practical. Knew so much better than my dusty cosseted elders who didn't know what it was like to really *feel*.

Now I know that where I really grew up was that library. Kindness insulated me from anything I didn't want to understand. I thought the past was still going, *humanity* was still going. You just had to believe.

Truly, my lumpy-headed daughter represented a break from all that came before. Just not in the blindly hopeful way Mai and I had intended.

'Come on, Daddy! Can't stand around dreaming, night'll getcha.'

My good girl dispelling the gloom, her short legs churning as they propelled her ahead. Already in action, knowing what we needed, she pushed her way in through the front doors. Dismissing the atmosphere as she'd shrugged off the miasma of the entire district. Nobody had given two hoots about locking this place.

We dropped the sled in the lobby and I let Flora dance on ahead to lead an investigation up the stairwells. Straight-faced pretending I hadn't already ruined my spine clearing it yesterday. It was essential she master survival habits; and as I'd learned the hard way, a small child with nothing to occupy her was a disaster.

Our footfalls crunched and slid in loose dry grit, like the

surface of a desert. Leaving tracks that would probably stay forever when we left. Floor after floor of blank rooms. Like nobody had ever subsisted cheek to jowl in these airless shoeboxes. Most of the plaster lay in chunks on the floor: good for us, let us get to the crannies behind. That's where the action would be.

I knew there was nobody to hear; still, the cheery 'Safe!' Flora chirped after poking her head into every damned doorway echoed maddeningly. By the second floor I was biting my cheek 'til it bled.

Huffing and puffing at the top, she eagerly waited for me to catch up and deliver the critical component to the whole performance: her pat on the head. Once I obliged, she positively glowed.

'Job well done, honey.'

I *did* feel proud. Didn't take time to tell her often enough, maybe. Dismissing the abundance of now "officially safe" rooms, we returned to the ground floor and began setting up.

A proper fire was on the cards tonight. Our most useful tool. And unlike those claustrophobic boxes hanging above our heads, the reception area was cross-ventilated so we wouldn't choke in our sleep.

Too easy a way to go. As I learned the hard way the night Mai yanked me out of our shelter, crying and slapping my numb cheeks, and struggling over the burden of her swollen belly.

Struggling awake was like trying to climb out of a pit, sleepy and clogged, as I laboured to comprehend my fuckup. My tent placement nearly suffocated us. We'd have burnt up or snorted down our oxygen. Pinched blue faces by dawn. Violet fingers and noses.

When I'd sobered up a bit I asked Mai what woke her. I

would have gone snoring into eternity. Frost was forming on my wife's lashes, her eyes huge and fervent and dark. She'd been waiting for that question. Put a hand on her stomach.

'Baby wants to live even more than we do.'

Mai felt nothing but awe, awash in the blessing of our child. Always the brave one. I had to look away, wracked with superstitious chills where I should have been grateful.

I could only think about how close to the edge we had come. And how comfortable it had been.

Flora and I raised our cosy tarpaulin pond in the most sheltered corner, behind what had been a security desk. The intact lobby doors were encouraging. I still secured them with loose brick to block drafts, and prevent the nocturnal wind flinging them about. Knowing our luck tonight would be the night they'd break.

For a while as we made ready the looming sky shouted orange through the panes. When I went to lookie-loo the snakes of pavement rust glowed in that light, livid and unworldly. As though the neighbourhood had been lashed for sins I couldn't imagine.

With the sun slumping outside, in the cinderblock clutch of the lobby the little poop-patty fire I constructed didn't seem too impressive. Its flickering light barely kissed the walls. Success was in the eye of the beholder, though, you didn't need much. In such a tall chimney of a building even body heat might've done the job—given more time than we had.

Wind began to rattle the doors, and intense cold to radiate in from outside. Now that night was on the way we were committed. So long as we steered clear of the glass our valiant fire burned, and the air gradually warmed.

First a tinkling and cracking, like delicate ice underfoot. It came from all around us, at the furthest reach of the light.

We grabbed our bachelor-curtain nets. Bugging eyes trying to be everywhere at once. Plaster crumbs pattered to the floor. Flora and I spun in dizzy circles seeking the noise. The shadows were untrustworthy. I felt so tight I wanted to scream, 'Come on!'

Miniscule bristles came poking out of the walls, the ceiling, until the tired old surfaces seethed. Chitin legs emerging, testing the air. The dormant insects were hatching.

'Go, honey, go, go, go!'

Flora obeyed, but squealed.

'They're biting me!'

Me too. Instead of slashing nails through my skin 'til it was bloody I clenched my teeth manfully and whirled the net around my head. What swarmed out of the dripping walls were small repulsive biting things. A thousand crawlings, a thousand unclean pinpricks. Feeding on us even as we harvested them. I couldn't stand it.

'Keep going Flora.'

She kept on, brave little soldier. All the while, her sobbing expressed what Daddy bit back.

Between us we cleared every room, every speck we could get. I couldn't tell what sort of bugs these were. Maybe some variety of blood-drinking, flying asshole ant. Like most ants they'd need to be toasted, or dinner would be like trying to crunch a mouthful of sour glass.

Anything with spines, I burned them off—could be toxic, or lodge in your tongue. A batch that looked unpalatable, or wriggling specks too small to manage; or, like this bonanza, both; we'd grind into flour for making flat biscuits. The taste generally came out lemon or nutty. Crumbled on the tongue, but didn't offend so long as there was water about.

Like content fishermen by our flickering fire we sat scraping tiny winged dots from our nets, shaking them from under ragged fingernails. And for the sake of awkward silence, I said, 'We're catching up to Alfred again.'

Flora's face had returned to rigid neutrality, over the nastiness of the harvest. Now her eyebrows drew infinitesimally closer.

'Alfred?'

'The man we're chasing, honey. The other father.'

Strange I hadn't mentioned before. Perhaps this nickname was a new conceit, my sense of time skewed.

'I call him "Alfred" cause he's kinda stooped. Like I imagine a butler would be.'

I demonstrated, shuffling as though carrying a silver tray. My shadow seemed alright. The resemblance was probably more convincing seen in silhouette, from a distance, as you were running.

Flora sat and sceptically turned my performance this way and that in her head, trying to decide how it fit in the shape of her world. Her hands always busy.

'What's the boy's name?' she asked finally in her quiet voice.

I blinked, but of course she'd be more interested in the boy. He looked about her age. There's nothing youth loves so much as its own reflection romanticised.

'Charleston,' I said, making it up on the fly.

'Why Charleston?'

'Because he looks a little fancy for my taste.'

It was true. Even from so far away the son did look clean and sturdy. And happy.

I'd heard young Charleston laugh, once. On the day I first discovered them, when we began the gruelling chase.

I'd been out listlessly scouting. Dragging my feet because what's the point? I was never going to find anything. Still, one went through the motions, the routine ground on. Out of the blue—well, grey—an unguarded peal of childish laughter bounced its way between mangled frowning skyscrapers. Bounced right down the block to end up in my incredulous ears.

At first I thought it was probably Flora—but she'd never made any kind of sound like that. So wild and carefree. Then I supposed I might be hallucinating. I'd long concluded we must be the last people alive; but it'd be weird to give up hope.

A glimpse of the other father, way off in the distance, put paid to that theory. My first look. Unaware of my existence, he was dawdling his son in the air, for the sake of hearing him laugh for joy. *Here comes the aeroplane*, when all the aeroplanes were gone.

I ought to have been thrilled to spot another human being. However this was the real world, not a bedtime story. They looked so carefree playing up there in the light, as though there was no risk. The small rotten vine of opportunity blossomed in my heart.

Pulse hammering a thousand times a second I sprinted back to the shelter to collect Mai and our things. And a weapon. I was going to need a weapon.

Flora nodded solemnly to such nonsense like I was telling a proper history. They were all disordered bedtime rhymes to her, her wacky parents and the times before Flora. I didn't want her forming her own narratives. Quick to supplant my own.

Pasting on a big fake smile, I played one of our games. It was something of a cruel game, which I reasoned away by saying a young girl needed things to look forward to.

'What will you ask when we catch them, honey?'

A question of unexpected gravitas this time. Perhaps because our quarry suddenly had names, a whole new dimension. I kept at my buggy work and didn't rush her, fascinated by the adult way she mulled it over.

Eventually Flora nodded to herself with adorable firmness, and ventured, 'I think I'll ask Charlie …'

'Charleston.'

'… what his favourite bugs are!'

So innocent; but I suddenly had to ask myself if the other father was even eating insects? His boy looked too strong, too healthy. Everything that Flora was not.

Briefly the urge to rip Alfred's secret from him was so intense I nearly sprinted right out those doors. Out of the lobby and into the killing night.

Instead I lowered my eyes, breathing hard until it passed. When I could face my daughter again my smile felt malformed and slipping. She didn't need to be bothered by Daddy's silliness.

'Well, sweetie, what if he asks you the same thing? What are *your* favourite bugs?'

Flora rolled her eyes. A startling gesture in that frozen face.

'Dad-*dee*! Grasshoppers, of course!'

She did her best squeaky imitation of their *skreep-skreep*.

Grasshoppers. Of course. We only found grasshoppers once. In the stub of a snapped off office block that hadn't looked promising. As someone who should have known not to judge a book by its cover, I'd nonetheless been resigned to going hungry.

What I wasn't prepared for was the harvest of fat vivid bodies that'd been coaxed forth by our fire. Didn't have the nets ready or anything. Had to scramble. One of the precious creatures landed on the back of my hand of its own accord with an elastic snap. Those towering back legs folded up while it decided where it wanted to go next.

Grinning incredulously, I held Senor Grasshopper up before Flora's face for inspection. One huge dark eye peered up at Flora, the other at me.

'Look, honey. This colour. This is what grass looked like. The world must've been a different place when this critter went to sleep.'

A garden world. Before the locusts that walked on two legs. Forestalling further conversation, the grasshoppers began to sing. In a way that made my eyes sting, even as I scooped the generous bounty. The whole broken tooth of a structure ringing with hymns to lost summer.

Measly by comparison, our current haul. We were exhausted enough to try a couple of uncooked mouthfuls: gritty and crunchy, blackening the teeth. Chewing close to the fire we had enough surplus warmth to strip and check each other for frostnip, skin issues, sunburn.

The sun was a curse. You'd stand in it, desperate to suck some warmth through your skin, but it remained tantalisingly cold and distant. Later, the burns. And hooray, we could now add itchy scratchy bug bites to our woes.

A damp cloth furnished a post-check wash, held frequently to the fire so it wouldn't freeze. The process left skin ruddy and lit astounded nerve endings up like fire, like ice. Pure silvery pain. Flora hated it and unveiled her rack of bird bones grudgingly.

When my daughter stood plumped up by clothes it was easy to forget how little of her there was. Now as she peeled herself free I was briefly victim of a waking nightmare that once all wrappings were removed there'd be nothing within. Silly Daddy. The firelight often lent itself to disordered thought.

My girl's grizzling aside, for me the wash was a relief. An opportunity for inventory. Sensation returned to reassure me that all extremities were still reporting for duty, fit to fight another day. Youth's foolishness was why Flora preferred to take that for granted, merely to avoid a little pain. She'd never witnessed the curled brown alternative rotting off a living limb.

I sported great overdeveloped legs from a decade of walking. The long muscles twitched rather grotesquely, more comfortable on the move than at rest; and didn't I know it trying to turn in of a night. Arms weren't up to much, though. Bones sawing their way through.

'Rawr!' I barked at Flora, pretending to be a T-Rex.

Predictably that went down like a lead balloon, as she'd no idea what a Tyrannosaurus was. Daddy's gone nutty. In the end, the crinkled label off a tin of dino-tastic spaghetti shapes with fifty percent more carnivore came to the rescue.

I hoarded labels from packets and cans for as long as I could before burning them, for quieter moments such as this when I could teach Flora to read. "Quiet" being subjective with the night wind blasting the building and rattling doors in a frenzy, but we took what we could get. Sounding out, 'Di-no-saur. Spa-ghe-tti.' Both extinct.

The best I could say was that Flora didn't seem to mind. Passing on culture was merely another chore, like melting water or assembling the pond. Becoming quite the little typeface expert but none of it set her on fire. Hard to believe she was my child, labouring over her letters. Reading had been *everything* to me at that age. The vanished world more vibrant and alive than the one around me.

Lastly before nighty-night I combed our sparse patchy hair with the special lice comb, a real treasure. Let Flora suck the result off the tines. Not much of a dessert, but no calories were too small for my girl.

It was during the night that we fell sick.

The screaming woke me first.

The wind was slamming about with its usual racket. Lulling, really, if you were used to it. This was something new buried in the noise, so high-pitched it came whining in via enamel rather than ears. I flailed awake with my teeth vibrating.

Disoriented, blinking in the dimness of banked fire. Blessedly unaware during those initial moments of just how ill I really was. Kind sleep had hidden it from me, swimming just below the surface. I clasped my jaw—what was I listening to? Horrified ululations; like the moment the city's inhabitants had realised they were going to die. That there was no government, no community, no enduring human spirit to carry them through.

Flora was sobbing, too, making it harder to hear. Her bones were still forming. Did it ring louder?

'Is it the ghosts, Daddy? Are they going to eat us?'

I cursed my stupid ass for telling that story. I didn't know what the racket was, either, which made it infinitely more terrifying. No Daddy for me to look up to.

The screaming was constant, disorienting. Prevented me taking a rational breath to make sense of what was happening. Panic insisted a multitude must be writhing in the ruins outside, being tortured. They might be coming for us next.

Watery moonlight seeping in through the glass doors suggested a lit floorshow of the torments in progress. I had to see. Sluggish and baffled, I tried to heave off my blankets.

That's when my stomach sank razor teeth in. The forlorn hope of my asshole clamped shut, with only minor success. By the hysteria of Flora's laments I figured the same was breaking out over there.

Sickness rippled up and down my hot skin, waves rocking me from side to side. My head had gone stuffed and loopy with fever. The last thing I wanted was to deal with her; could scarce manage to lie panting shallowly. Enough to try and keep my incandescent skull from splitting as awfulness pulsed out the other end. On any other day it'd be a source of profound shame.

Our mistake, harvesting so far inside the industrial district. And weren't we paying for it.

—*we had to eat*—

Sure. Perhaps the building's refrain had been the same, floor by floor, as teratomas flourished and babies were pushed into the world with no arms. *We have to live somewhere.* Who could weigh an invisible curse, when all the choices have already been made for you?

I mustered the strength to roar, 'Would somebody stop that damn screaming so I can think!'

Immediately exhausted by the effort. Exhausted by the violent uptick in my daughter's crying, and the way nothing ever went right. I was a limp rag on the tile. But if a rag could roar, it could drag itself along.

'Dad-dee.' From behind me. 'Please. I feel sick.'

I ought to crawl back. My Flora was crying out for me. So was the maddening screaming, coming from outside to scramble my brain, and if it was with my last breath I intended to witness the crime.

I heaved myself to the lobby doors. Into the orbit of their bitter cold, which made me recoil like a salted slug before pressing on. Felt like I'd crossed an entire desert. I rested my inflamed brow on the glass, expecting the pane to flash into steam. Huffs of breath frosting my view. I peered out.

A gravid moon hung massively over a scene that ought to have been tossing and rocking with the volume of wind pouring through it. This neighbourhood was clearly old collapse; anything likely to shift had been scoured off long ago right down to the dirt. The clashing motionlessness and fury lent an untrustworthy aspect.

I certainly didn't trust what I was seeing. My mental equilibrium had been troubling for some time, ever since striking out on my own with Flora to take care of. Now look what was happening. My fever-cooked senses made me think I saw the circle of cheap apartment buildings restored, limned in stark moonlight.

No longer alone, our shelter took its place among its lost brothers and sisters. And those balconies! Laddered up to the heavens—if I could cower any more, sink through the floor, I would have. Clasped both hands horrified over my face as though I could hide.

The old residents' faces peered down at me from all those balconies. *I* was the floor show, the living interloper and they couldn't wait to take a peek. Not just the final group who died here, curled in the miserable cold beneath beds, inside cupboards, anywhere they could hide. All those who'd been consigned to this unsuitable place. Ever since the cheap block had been thrown up to make somebody else a buck. Residents overlapping, blurring.

You can bet whoever profited from the construction died somewhere warm. Food to the end. If anybody deserved to be resurrected into this purgatory it was *them*.

I had no doubt I was seeing this now because Flora and I were so close to joining the residents' association. Their eyes hollowed away to wisps of hair behind.

And those mouths. Long funnelling tunnels for the wailing wind. Those mouths extended in fleshy loops down from the balconies toward the play equipment huddled below, like a sea of vines, to blast it and make it scream. The only voice they had left.

I turned my head resolutely. I never saw that.

'It's just the wind,' I called to Flora. 'There's nobody out there, honey. No ghosts. Only the play equipment making noise as the wind blows through.'

The pitch rose angrily, to counter my platitudes. The glass itself shivered beneath my forehead. The residents did not fancy being denied, they'd had enough of that in life. We were already being bad neighbours. Good. I'd no intention of joining them.

We needed water, and lots of it. To wash as well as to hydrate. Ironic how deadly cold it was out under that swollen moon, yet here we were burning up in here. I was lying on the floor with sweat pouring out.

Not to mention the unmentionables that were still threatening to burst forth, my asshole apparently not wrung dry enough for all it felt like old rubber. Standing was out of the question. Anything I wanted to accomplish would have to be done face-down.

Get to it, Jim. Frost off the panes of glass for melting. The long miserable process of cleaning first Flora, then myself; trying not to gag because she was already crying. All the while shaking my head and refusing to glance back out at the lunatic scene. I never saw that.

Stoic in the embarrassment and discomfort because despite the cold's best efforts and unlike the miserable mob out there, we were still alive.

It came close to being the worst night of my life. The lacklustre dawn revealed the same ruined courtyard as yesterday. Our building forlorn and lonely. The play equipment squatted, staring back at me slyly. Waiting to sing.

Worse, as the light revealed us both waxen and shaking, I was faced with a terrible dilemma. Our sickness had been no fever-dream. We couldn't stay a second night while I staggered out to find us a safer bolthole.

The routine was shot. Panic gripped me (gently, I couldn't tolerate much squeezing). I started this way and that, packing, pacing, unable to choose a direction.

Flora had come to the same conclusion.

'I have to come with you, Daddy. I can't stay behind.'

'Baby ...'

'I'm not a baby anymore.'

That made me smile, right over the top of all the fear and worry. Pride splitting my heart right open. She could barely stand but by God when Flora intended to do something she would do it.

'Of course you are, honey. You're *my* baby.'

We had a way forward. Leave this building to fall down and join its brethren, the play equipment to howl to no-one. Lost lives to go unremembered. We were going to make it.

And once again, I vowed to do better. My brave Flora would be the one good thing in my life I deserved.

FLORA & JIM

Chapter Three

Sweet Home

IF SPARKS HADN'T broken out at the settlement we'd have slogged right on by.

Fortunately on such a breathless day smoke soars straight up. An oily roiling exclamation point. Conspicuous as a shout in a landscape that amounted to no more than a vast, gently undulating reflection of the featureless clouds. Where any direction felt like walking nowhere. Once upon a time, these had been suburbs.

Places of resource like urban centres belonged to the hidden animals now, the new landlords. Humans had been pushed out to marginal bits. If there were any more of us left.

With Flora stepping lively on point I'd indulged, trudging half-asleep with head dangling. My thoughts didn't exist beyond the ache circling my narrow shoulders. The grooves went a finger deep where the sled harness had cut in and made itself at home.

No doubt when I expired my scattered bones would testify to an adult life as a beast of burden. Chunked in deformed knots. Bowed and thinned elsewhere.

My daughter made a noise between a snort and a yelp. That snapped my head up right quick, too quick, fresh jolts of pain neck to skull. Worried she'd tripped or fallen or God knows what. Seizures were a thing of the past, although sometimes she vagued out. Mai would have loved to hear she'd been right. We made it this far, and our shaking little baby was growing into something new.

Flora was still safe on her feet. I stumped up beside to grump.

'What do you see?'

Her eyesight was so much better than the slow betrayal of mine. The lack of tall buildings didn't guarantee safe terrain out here and I missed the city.

'Smoke!'

Now I clocked the stark pillar, too, and felt a bit silly for asking. Would have gotten there a lot sooner had I been walking with my brain switched on.

Smoke meant fire, suggested people. A once in a lifetime opportunity I had solid grownup reasons for not wanting to rush. Nonetheless, I welcomed the burr in our smooth routine. Too often my Flora seemed tied up in troubles that were none too cheery and, more alarmingly, none of my beeswax.

I didn't fancy these signs of a mournful interior life. Given all I'd done for her it didn't seem right to hide things. What's so bad that a girl can't tell her Daddy?

'Anything else, honey?'

'Under.'

Flora answered shortly, shading her eyes and squinting to study it. Or was she making a show of not looking at me? Out here *everything* was below street level. Structures pushed over, frost the new ground.

'Smallish.'

Apparently we were feeling monosyllabic today. She was right, though. Our beacon already raggedy, having spent its fuel.

'Hm. That's the direction our good pals Alfred and Charleston headed in.'

Flora perked up.

'Really?'

'Would I lie to you, baby? Wonder if they touched it off being careless.'

Flora and I were moving more swiftly together instead of in one-two hops; canny Alfred had scented *that* game, and altered his habits accordingly. Still, the other father couldn't elude me. My daughter's eyes might be superior, but my very blood would seek him out.

'Are we going down there, Daddy? Might be stuff we can use?'

—*well now, suddenly the little Shakespeare*—

I stared glumly at the stutters of smoke, chewing my lip. What further risks? How far would I go to keep Flora happy? Typically, that was the worst question I could have asked myself.

As it turned out, what had been on fire was the entryway to a settlement. Tucked into what'd been a shallow underground cark park. A good position—prime. So cunningly socked away that even with Flora's eagle eye we'd have surely trotted on, oblivious. Which would have been exactly how the homemakers liked it.

Although smoke no longer streamed out, the passage reeked of soot. The entrance was a series of doglegs airlocked by hanging blankets through which the smoke had to twist and wend to escape.

—*other people*—

The thought rushed through, hot and then cold; leaving me faintly sick. I entered first, for all the good it would do. Wanted to holler, 'Hello?' in case they were friendly, but what the hell kind of example would that set for my girl.

Not a peep from within the nest. Another kind of smell leaked out, though, beneath the acrid burning. Just as incriminating. Unwashed folk crammed together, all farting, coughing, burping, sweating, and generally living their lives. Flora coughed in disgust.

'People live here,' I muttered back to her so she wouldn't be shocked when we emerged inside. 'Lots of people. I grew up somewhere very similar.'

'How many is lots?'

'Well, there were ten of us in the Family, counting me. Ten's plenty. This could have been one of their outposts, if they'd had any.'

The Family. I didn't think I'd remember as much as I did. All that richness and warmth, all they'd done and all I'd done, shelved as no longer relevant. Forgetting was easy. To go dredging it up, now we might actually have a use for social niceties, was harder.

Flora of course was agog, as with any topic touching on others. Mythic people. Somebody not her, or her Dad, or a vague maybe-figure we pursued into the distance. Practically a unicorn.

'And including Mum?'

'Yes ... of course. Ten of us, plus your Mum.'

—*mai came later. everything changed*—

'Who were they?'

Back on safer ground. I held up fingers.

'There was Aunt Abena, she was in charge. And her brother Uncle Ebo. He loved to cook, his favourite way of looking after people. Uncles Isaiah and Alessio. And Aunts Paisley, Makayla, Isla, Aaliyah, and Amelia.'

'Why so many Aunts?'

'You know, I asked Aunt Amelia that very same question. She was the oldest person who ever existed, which made her pretty smart. She told me men wear out faster.'

'You're not going to wear out, though, are you Daddy?'

A spike of guilt for causing her worry. Especially as on bad days I felt like I was already there.

'No, sweetheart. Daddy's every bit as tough as Aunt Abena, and she could open cans with her bare hands! Hooboy, you did not cross Abena.'

'That's why she was in charge?'

'That's right. Abena the warrior. Love her or hate her, she made everybody feel safe. And if you were lost she'd always come and find you.'

'Always?'

'Well. You know. If you *wanted* to be found.'

Not long after we came upon what remained of the fire. The entryway's innermost hanging had burned fitfully, a nose-stinging smoulder that suggested human hair in the weave. I'd never thought of that. And Flora's hair was coming in nicely, a whole headful of resource we were growing for free.

On that final turn my foot crashed through something on the floor and almost made me jump out of my skin. Holding the scorched shreds of blanket out of the way I knelt for closer examination.

It had been the charred remains of a small tepee of splinters: kindling, more precious than gold; from which the hanging had caught. My clumsiness scattered the fragile tableau into the blank space within the car park. So dark and quiet in there. Still, I pocketed what I could.

This felt weird. I didn't like weird. The fire that drew us had been deliberately and wastefully lit: to what purpose? And if this *was* a settlement, where was everybody? Could they be hiding?

Visions of the other father scuttling in to warn them, like a rat slipping down a hole. All of them scurrying in the dark. Waiting to leap out, and not to yell, 'Happy birthday!' It was not a pleasant image.

I put my lips to Flora's ear, careful not to risk a decibel more than necessary.

'We're gonna need the lamp, honey.'

My good girl didn't argue. Spun straight around to go back out to the sled. I listened to her retreating footsteps, the soft *woomph* of blankets pushed aside. Wealth, all these blankets, so much better than anything we carried. Imagine being able to weave or reweave with such skill.

Aunt Aaliyah tried to show me the basics. Out of duty more than affection, I suspect; she'd have loved a niece instead of a clumsy inattentive nephew to pass her skills on to. It was to her credit I was able to sew at all. Can't learn that from a book.

I ought to have cautioned Flora to return before sparking the damn lamp up, one fire was plenty. Shouldn't have worried. She came carefully, lifting the hangings well clear. The light was a comfort already; Flora hesitated before surrendering it when I held my hand out.

I held the lamp high and we stepped forward into the settlement.

The inside was a fair bit squeezier than the exterior had suggested. Low ceiling, of course, standard cost-saving construction. Also because of how thickly they'd insulated the walls with whatever came to hand. A familiar technique, but the Family's efforts had been ... different.

Aunt Paisley always kept the brightest scraps and loveliest colours for the inner layer. Hours of work fitting and hanging for the sake of a brief happiness, a kaleidoscope that pleased the heart.

I'd tried to replicate her art in my own small way with the pond. Wanted Flora to open her eyes to pleasure, even if our teeth rattled and hair froze to our pillows.

These were nothing but piles of unsorted rags up to the cramped ceiling. Dull, streaked in mud, they made the walls crowd inward. Ready to avalanche down. A soft unclean *ploomph* and we'd be crushed flat as a tack.

I had to remind myself not to rasp, idiot, there's plenty of air.

—*you'll panic flora—*

My daughter had removed her balaclava and outer layer while I stared around and daydreamed. Realising my scalp prickled with sweat I rapidly scraped mine off, too. The warm stuffy air sent sparks dancing in extremities. Folk had been here alright, and not so long ago that the heat had seeped away.

'Where I grew up was nicer than this.'

I spoke in a hushed voice as we shone the lamp about the abandoned space, because I didn't want Flora thinking this dismal hole was how it had been.

'The Family were all fairly old and without kids of their own ... anymore. But they made a big effort to create a loving home for any they came across. It was part of their ... well, creed, I guess. Not that they found many children. For a long time it was just me.'

We clambered among vague pillars of rags cladding the support columns: knotted faces, cloth sneers. Flora's blank features swivelled like a radar dish, daring anything to ambush us out of the dark.

—don't you hurt my daddy—

'People get too old to have kids? Are you too old?'

'Ha—your Pa's got sauce in him yet, honey. But why on earth would I want another baby? You're already perfect.'

I was baiting to provoke 'I'm not a baby!' but she didn't rise. Wrong atmosphere for levity. So I went on.

'In hindsight I guess not all the Family were too old. They looked older than the hills to me at the time, but I was no bigger than you, then. Avoiding having any more children of their own was a sort of group decision they arrived at. Or peer pressure decision, if you listened to Aunt Paisley. She was bitter that Aunt Abena had already had her turn, it was easy for her to draw the line.'

'Why wouldn't they want kids?'

With her forlorn tone Flora might as well have asked, 'What's wrong with me?'

I made a conscious effort to unknot my fists. Silly how even after all this time the echo of old resentment combined with my fresh modern grief to unman me.

'Because so far as they saw things, there was no future. With varying degrees of fervour the Family believed the world was becoming a sort of frozen hell. And it was humanity's duty, our dignity, to die out peacefully. While we were still civilised. The full name they used was The Last Family.'

As the adult here, I probably could have filtered this information better for Flora's level of understanding. Instead, I'd been holding it in so long that it came pouring out of me in a bitter torrent, just as it'd come to me from them. Strong emotions never communicate well. Up to my daughter, then, to do her best with it. As I had.

Flora made a scornful little snort, sharing my sentiment in her limited way.

'The last? Mum came. Now there's us.'

'Exactly! There's your future for you. The day they brought your mother home, and I'd say neither Mai or I were much older than you are now, was the day I *knew*, just *knew* all that no-future talk was a lie. I mean, I'd been reading about the old world all my life. How could that just be gone? Why *couldn't* we build a new one? Big beginnings from small things.'

Blankness appraised me.

'How old am I?'

So spindly, my sticks and straw girl. Small things indeed. I took a punt. Made it sound confident.

'Twelve-ish.'

Ok, so not as firm as I was hoping but apparently twelveish would do. In the wavering light Flora silently absorbed that, appending it to the list of facts she knew about herself. All catalogued by me.

'Twelve was well old enough for me to see what was so magical about your mother. I was no idiot.'

Well "no idiot" was debatable. Enchanted, yes, by that first glimpse of Mai's round smiling cheeks. Walking demurely between scouts Makayla and Paisley as they escorted her in through the door.

Only that wasn't right. I had yet to glimpse Mai's face, and she couldn't have been smiling in that rose-tinted moment because she'd been carried in, one Aunt at her shoulders and the other with her feet. Howling in rage and grief for her real family, who were most likely icicles out in the cold. That's how you ended up with the Family. Howling like a maddened animal.

Mai gave gentle old Aunt Makayla a black eye before they even made it through the doorway. Couldn't have made a better choice, or a worse one. Makayla didn't have it in her to hold any kind of grudge, but others did. It didn't win Mai any friends. Now, if it'd been *Uncle Isaiah* who she'd walloped the Aunts would have applauded.

Makayla tried to explain it to me later in her whispery voice, as she winced and dabbed her eye with a washcloth in the mirror.

'People do odd things in the grip of sorrow, Jim. Odd and profound things. Don't hold it against the girl. She'll need a friend, if she's to get over it.'

The Family were all like that. Patience wrapped in papery skin, absorbing misfortune as just due. I couldn't stand it. I was the only one excited and disturbed by the newcomer. The rest merely … dumped her in a room and went about their day.

Only now I think they might have been trying to set an example for me. Wasted, obviously. Such being the fate of high horses and high hopes.

Oh, Mai. What a revelation, exploding into my sheltered world. Fight and fire. Me, eager tinder, and I had yet to even see her face.

'What was Mum like, when she was like me?'

That brought on a smile. Against the mood of the moment, but Flora sounded so *much* like Mai.

'Same as you, love. Full of questions. The Family seemed stuffy and old-fashioned, happy enough their world worked at all, if only for a little longer. That wasn't enough for Mai. Drove her nuts, actually.

'She was all for the how, the why, and can anything be done better. Constantly poking, like, why didn't we take over that other building, spread out? Like the Aunts and Uncles weren't lonely enough already in their uneasy balance of proximity and personal space to mourn.

'Basically, Mai never fit in. And it was only after meeting her I realised that I didn't either. I never had.'

Unnerving, that realisation. When I'd known one home all my life, my shape worn in. A rut, Mai called it. Never saw the point of a comfortable groove.

Ugh, I'd been drifting in my thoughts again. Flora was waiting for more.

'You've definitely got your mother's eyes, honey. Look at you, all bright and bushy-tailed, peering up at me. Little curious eyes.'

—too much, too much of her in you—

Those eyes, in a face less rigid and cold. Plump instead of skeletal. A face that'd been built for emotion of any stripe, so long as it lit the world on fire. Those eyes had once enraptured me as the snake charms the mongoose.

The door to Mai's room remained closed. I found excuses to walk past all week. Uncle Isaiah, who was fond of exactly the number of folk who reciprocated (zero), grumbled, 'Girl'll come out when she's hungry enough. Quit treating her like a princess, or she'll never settle in.'

Fat chance I was going to do anything *he* suggested. I left offerings on the mat outside, lit saintly blue and crimson by my candy-wrapper lantern. My old night-haunts would just have to deal with themselves; I had another fascination now. And a feeling this girl might be grappling with terrors of her own.

Uncle Ebo wasn't about to chastise me for the pilfered treats; I knew he worried about the newcomer as well. And seeing as it was his kitchen and he was Abena's brother, nobody else dared say boo. I must have gone through, twenty, thirty candles. Crazy wasteful.

Aside from my impromptu little shrine on the stoop, no outward indication that this bedroom was unique. Silent as a tomb in there. Not a peep. So many rooms in the home with identical shut doors, prepared for the comfort of children who never came.

A dreadful snoop, I knew how wretchedly Aunt Paisley wept in the night, guilty we'd been unable to find them. It's why she volunteered for the uncomfortable, dangerous work of being a scout. Well, perhaps our newcomer would cheer her up. If the feisty girl was even still alive in there.

Now an adult familiar with the conscience's tricks I wonder if in those late hours, in some corner of Aunt Paisley's soul, all the babies of the world were still trapped and suffering under the snow. The rubble abounded with infants crying out for her.

Including the one she'd wished so hard for herself. That was why she couldn't sleep when the rest of the home was quiet, and lifted weights instead. Working to drown out the cries. They could still be saved if she just ... did ... better.

I should have been nicer to Aunt Paisley.

I'd almost given the new girl up. Was visiting glumly by rote rather than hope when the door flew unexpectedly open and a face lunged out of the dark at me.

A crunch underfoot, that was the end of my delicate harlequin lantern. All I caught were wide staring eyes and a rictus mouth rushing me. I flung up both hands and ignominiously squealed. Landed a light accidental slap on her face.

—that was for aunt Makayla—

The girl seized me with fingers that felt like talons. Dragged me inside and slammed the door behind us.

It didn't smell too good in here. Shut-ins seldom do. Me, practically hyperventilating in the dark with a stranger I knew nothing about, and none of the Family knew where I was.

'You! Did they steal you too?'

'What? No—I'm Jim.'

The mental wheels weren't turning too well.

'Can I light the lamp?'

Forgetting it had been smooshed.

'Leave it off!'

'Look. You're safe here.'

A rude noise. Was she off to my left? I faced that direction.

'They probably went and fed you that line about your folks being dead, too, huh?'

'My parents *are* dead. Way before I could remember. Aunt Abena and Uncle Ebo are my parents now … sort of.'

'Well mine aren't! They stole me, Jim. They took me from my family.'

Put *that* in your pipe and smoke it.

'No.'

With my butt I pushed the door open. Blessed light! Began backing out of the room. I was afraid she'd come after me, but like a vampire the girl ducked deeper into the shadows.

'No, that can't be right.'

'Fine, side with them. Who needs you, anyway!'

'Who are you?' I asked desperately, trying to salvage anything. She was trying to shut me out.

A fierce eye through the gap in the door. A beautiful eye.

'Mai.'

Mai slammed it in my face.

Now I recognise Mai for what she was: a frightened, traumatised child lashing out. Trying to gain the upper hand any way she could. Survival depended on it. My heart aches for her.

But in the heat of the moment, to a kid no older with his head stuffed with fiction, she'd seemed unearthly. A goddess. Or a demon.

'Your mother had all her fingers and toes, too. Proof somebody loved her well before us.'

But surely, I thought, not more than I.

Turned out Uncle Isaiah was right, which happened often enough to make you want to scream. Mai emerged from her burrow eventually. Wasting away wasn't her style, not even in front of a brand new audience.

As it turned out she dreaded being alone. Would rather hover by somebody she loathed. That made integration about as good as you'd expect. We were all on death watch those first few weeks to prevent her running out into the cold, a stunt she only pulled knowing Aunt Abena would usher her back.

Despite my itch of curiosity it was difficult to engage on any level about her family, or what her life had been like. She'd fly into an unreasoning rage. 'My Dad'll get you!' was a plum favourite.

Early interest waned. For all their high ideals most of the Family stamped her with "brat" and left well enough alone. Returned to pursuing their own slow hobbies in mournful silence.

Initially, disdainful Mai didn't want any more to do with me than the rest. Warm bodies, that's all we were, so she didn't have to stew alone with her thoughts. It was months before she'd accept my overtures of friendship.

Our time passed, condensed for me into a series of triumphs and reversals. I learned she needed to win arguments. Let her take down the barrier between me and her parents' sacred memory at her own pace. Ignorant the whole time to the hard yards she was putting into her own agenda.

A full year on found us naughtily hiding from chores together. Mai's idea, as was the cupboard we were in. I quite liked chores, made me feel like I was contributing. With us crammed in so close and all I finally got up the guts to ask, 'How are you so sure your parents are still looking for you? I mean, after all this time?'

Mai's glare could have withered a girder.

'Uh, because they're my *parents*. If it was your kid you'd never give up, and you'd never stop looking. Even for years. It would be like some hole in your soul.'

Mai enjoyed a touch of the dramatic.

'That's what I have. A hole where my family should be.'

Now didn't seem the appropriate time to say that although they seemed cold, the Family would love her as they loved me, even if they didn't like her. Defend her with their lives. Die, even.

Besides, I'd already realised this was to no credit of Mai or myself. It was something to do with children in general. We represented a concept that couldn't be ignored—the future, I guess. Or lack thereof if you believed the Family's dogma.

Nonetheless I wanted to offer comfort. Let her know she was part of something special, at least to me, in a language she would hear. Now was the time to be bold. To be the anti-Jim.

I leaned forward, Mai's face swelling huge in my field of vision. Front row seat to her sudden alarm. And I kissed her for the very first time. It was a sharp blow to the heart from which I never recovered.

One chaste kiss, like a circuit closing. That echoed through my life, forward and back. Even now—sweet pain. I could close my eyes and feel the ripples.

I sat back on my heels, feeling a bit hormone-drunk.

Mai looked as shocked as someone hiding in a cupboard could be. Hm, maybe I'd read this wrong. The testosterone dose made me reckless—too late now!

She gathered her wits.

'Why did you do that?'

'I wanted you to feel better.'

—even now i cringe—

Momentum interrupted, but she got back on track.

'What's going to make me *feel better* will be getting back to my Mum and Dad. I'm going to make it; years, months, I don't care.'

A small curl at the corner of her mouth. The way she looked at me, as though really *seeing* me, made the edges of the cupboard bloom out.

'And you, Jim. You're going to help me.'

'Why'd you leave, if those folk took such good care of you?'

I swallowed, hard. So much to remember, and all coming down on top of me at once.

'Well, sweetheart, Mai and I didn't need to be taken care of anymore.'

That hardly encompassed the shame, exhilaration and terror. I'd already decided Flora didn't need any of that. For her I reserved the small bright gems. How our flight had briefly felt that we were running into a future of hope.

On a more prosaic note, Flora and I were also running out of car park. The rear wall loomed up and we'd found diddly. Still, suspicious eddies of cold air beat patty cake on my exposed cheeks. If we hadn't taken our balaclavas off I probably would've missed it.

Following the temperature gradient I pushed aside another hanging, thick as a carpet, and uncovered a broad ramp leading into even deeper darkness. Voila, the second level. If we were going to find anything worth having, looks like it would be downstairs.

Which really made my hair stand on end. I peered down the ramp uneasily. Heat rises, and as per normal the settlement's living space was up here where warmth was designed to be trapped, keep you safe. There shouldn't be anything down there but cold storage.

'Daddy. What's ..?'

Flora held aloft a tuft of something caught on the railing. A puff. Rough and greyish-white.

I leaned in for a look and my stomach bottomed out. Fur.

Reason wanted to pretend it'd torn from someone's clothes, perhaps as they ran to hide in the dark. Reason was an optimistic fool. The stifling heat closed in and I panted lightly through my mouth.

Don't panic. Couldn't afford to panic. Then Flora would panic, and we'd likely never see the sky again. Just be straightforward.

'Animals have been here, honey.'

And when she crouched in fright, I muttered, 'The Family had issues with animals, too.' To make her think this was old hat, I knew what to do.

Lies. Never like this. Never animals sneaking inside, past the fires and walls that made you feel safe. One last protected corner of the world to crawl into.

—never like this. except ... abena's son went missing—

When the earth turned cold, animals reacted like innovative geniuses. They might as well have been poised for it to happen.

Which was funny because humanity, gifted with foresight, wasted time blundering around disbelieving.

A flood of animals competing for the same limited resources really accelerated the process. For us hapless dwindling humans, already culled by temperature, it was like the lavish table of our ancestors was being devoured by ghosts in front of our eyes.

Again and again animals beat the Family's scouts to key food sources like buried supermarkets. Better at it every year. Each time the emptied useless remains were met with quiet humour. Like it was good, that beasts were pressuring people to die out faster. Brought the Family's endgame into sight.

As a child as much as an adult, the lighter side eluded me. The prospect of a growling belly was its own kind of ravenous beast. One that wouldn't listen to reason.

True first contact with Mai happened when she stumbled across me ... I guess you'd say "playing". Seemed dreadfully serious practice at the time. Lunging and stabbing the air with a sliver of sharpened metal.

'What are you doing?'

My chest swelled but I pretended to ignore her. Let the gentle doe come to you, urged the literature.

'I'm going to catch an animal.'

'No you're not.'

Instant, and so know-it-all. She infuriated me.

'I'm going to catch an animal and we're going to eat it.'

I showed her my carefully curated collection of books on the topic. Admittedly more cookery than field craft. Mai was watching me more closely than the pages. Like every little boy for the past thousand years I was pompously explaining the facts of life to a girl; but couldn't shake the unease that she was hearing something different than how marvellous I was.

Still I carried on. Classic little lad.

'I already know you've gotta hang the carcass upside down to drain the blood out. And you gotta be super-quick about taking out the … the poop parts, so's they don't poison the food bits.'

Waving the illustration under her nose, waiting for her to maidenly blanch from the graphic titillation. Instead I got impatience.

'That's ridiculous.'

She stabbed a finger at the page.

'Nobody's seen any animals. We don't even know what they look like anymore.'

I struck a pose and thrust boldly with my makeshift spear, *poke poke poke*.

'I know I can manage—once I find one. It's meant to be.'

Signs, I meant. I'd seen signs. A dream about snuggling down in warm fur. I dropped a mug, and the water splashed out in the shape of … some kind of quadruped.

Mai looked on, unimpressed.

'You'd be better off trying to conk it on the head or something. Before it bites your ass to bits.'

'They're just animals, and animals are all the same. Even us.'

Her eyes narrowed.

'Us?'

'Sure, we're animals, too. Animals who wear clothes and think we're special. And we haven't changed much.'

'Speak for yourself.'

Scepticism aside, thus began Mai's new hobby: trying to poke holes in my grand plans. I didn't mind—attention was attention. Told myself that in the courting dance it hardly mattered when I didn't know the correct answers to her challenges about survival outside. Only that I responded as confidently as some grizzled outdoorsman, knife clenched between my teeth.

Easy to prance about playing the expert when nobody can prove you wrong. If Mai had bothered fostering a relationship with the scouts, the real experts, we would certainly have had a different story.

'Animals like the goat?' Flora asked timidly.

The only animal she'd been exposed to. I didn't believe for one second that Flora remembered the goat. She remembered the goat I'd told her about.

'Sure, honey. Now, baby, I'm going to need you to go back to where we came in, by the blankets, and wait for me there.'

'No.'

'Flora …'

'*No*, Daddy.'

Eyes glimmering stressed white all the way around, belying the stubbornness of that frozen face.

'What if the animal gets you. Then I'll be all alone.'

I couldn't push the argument further without being louder than was safe. Pinned her with a glare Mai would've been proud of.

—*we'll discuss your behaviour later young lady*—

I had my daughter to lavish worry on. Who was relying on me to find food. That was plenty of grief for one man. In my little bubble of light I steeled myself and descended the ramp.

Concrete dust rolled and skidded underfoot. The air drawn over my teeth tasted silt, chalky. Couldn't have been nice for the residents to breathe. They ought to have swept up; although upstairs suggested cleanliness wasn't high on their agenda. Aunt Aaliyah would've hated that. She was always, *wash this, scrub that*. I'm sure she thought children carried disease.

Ventilation seemed sketchy, the lamp guttered with each step. I shielded it with my life because if the light went out and left us stranded down here, I couldn't guarantee I'd ever be able to stop shrieking. Flora trailed silently at the very rim of the lamp's influence. Great big solitary lit target, me.

In my catgut state of nerves it occurred belatedly to check for footprints. All I got was a crazy mess of scrapes, smears and drags. No funny waltzing here. The temperature dropped dramatically. This was how I'd always imagined wading into water must feel. Not so dangerous to life as venturing outside; I regretted leaving my outer layers by the entrance, though.

At least it gave me an excuse other than fear to shiver. Down we went. And the dust turned to icy red mud, reflecting a ruddy glow back into our horror-struck faces.

Had I thought my heart was hammering before? Now slamming around my chest, demanding that I run. It was gore underfoot. Frozen solid enough to walk on. Flora's breath hitched and I knew she'd seen, oh my poor little girl.

—*wish you'd done as you were told now, honey?*—

I wished I'd waited by the entrance. Wasn't an option for me.

We reached the lower level. B1 stencilled in yellow on every big round exposed support pillar, for "Basement One". And the blood went on forever. The entire floor, as the struggle had surged across the room.

Spackled up the walls. Thin finger stalactites of it descended from the ceiling, pointed accusingly at the mess below. Who could look at this and claim anyone had wanted to live more than these people.

Whoever they'd been, they'd been doing much better than the Family. More than ten souls, that was for sure. I was right, this had been a storage area. A place of bounty for the thriving if stinky community above. Plenty for a nice, robust future.

Metal shelves, that must have been dragged in from some warehouse, had been toppled in the struggle. Open cans were strewn everywhere. Every tin emptied, of course. Animals couldn't read a label but knew there was a chance of food inside. Each of the quick-evolving winners must sport a specialised claw, beak, or tooth.

Opening cans was the least of it. By the state of the churned floor it looked like they'd opened up every human being as well. So *much* blood. Any trace of other tissue, even bone, had been licked away while still warm. How had I fancied I could kill one on my own, when even fierce Aunt Abena had never managed the feat?

I swallowed and risked shutting my eyes briefly to pray there'd been no children. Were I struck down in that unguarded breath, it would have to be the price I paid for hanging on to my humanity.

For Flora's sake I was glad for the absence of bodies. And, shamefully, on my own behalf. I remembered the motorcyclist trembling beneath the stripped sky, the sheer amount of *meat* on him. In these lean times I was thankful not to be tested.

Still we had to search. I pretended it might be for survivors, when really I was scratching around for some scrap to have been overlooked. A single can out of all this, surely, somewhere. We could load up on a wealth of blankets, but we couldn't eat them.

Flora looked like she wanted to levitate to avoid touching any contaminated surface. She gave up halfway and stood against a wall fiddling with something. I thought I saw a flash of paper and brought the lamp over.

'What have you found, honey?'

She showed it to me sheepishly.

'Must've belonged to Charlie, huh?'

Not paper, my eyes were playing tricks. A perfectly good plastic bottle. Alfred must have known we'd pick it up. The prospect of taking his leavings soured my mouth. My only consolation, the terrible things he must have done to be so successful.

'Leave it.'

'But Daddy ...'
'Leave it!'
'Why?'

Flora was putting on a brave front but hectic roses bloomed in her cheeks. This grim place must be affecting her more than I thought. I tried to lighten the mood.

'What will you ask them when we catch up?'

The roses spread.

'Nothing!' Flora snapped fiercely. 'Cause they'll be too busy trying to murder us, or us them. Isn't that how it goes?'

I was taken aback, literally backing three steps away. She sounded like Mai.

'Honey ...'

'That's how it *is*! But they helped us, Dad. Charlie set the fire so's we'd see all this, to warn us.'

'Honey, you don't know that.'

'He did!'

Too furious for further words Flora stamped her way back up the ramp. Flabbergasted, I let her go. She wasn't silly enough to wander too far.

I didn't want to admit it could be true. The nearest possibility was that young Charleston might've set off the signal in secret, without his father's blessing. It would explain the prodigious waste of kindling. Risking so much to reach out to sworn enemies made him a better man than me. This basement, this bloodied horror, I wouldn't wish this on anyone. I repaid with my sincere hope that duplicity uncovered, Alfred had yelled up one side of Charleston and down the other.

Flora credited the boy, clearly. She had such a good heart. Sometimes I think our two children will grow into such beautiful young people. Face to face for the first time on an open plain, stirred by a fresh breeze, Flora and Charleston will smile shyly and hold out their hands in friendship.

Fanciful heaven, I suppose. Even imagine tundra flowers; ragged stubborn clumps of swaying colour. In this fantasy Alfred and I are already dead. Swollen bug-eyed corpses with fists locked about each other's throats. Left behind in some long-forgotten place much like this one, because how else could this end?

An unusually smooth patch at my feet flickered. A thick puddle, like a scarlet mirror. Somebody had perished right where I was standing. The motion caught my eye; I shuddered and scuffed my boot over it before I'd fully processed what I'd seen.

For a confused instant I caught the reflection of a round-cheeked face that couldn't be mine. Fatigue fleshed the mirage with wide-staring eyes. And a rictus mouth growing as it lunged at me. Frozen as though screaming.

—*jim! something's …—*

In truth I fear she was laughing.

I fled back up the ramp to get away, plunging into the warmth of the upper level. Like a miser I took light with me, plunged the fate of the settlement and all who'd tried to make their future here back into darkness.

Rubbing my arms to dispel gooseflesh as thoroughly as memory. I'd seen nothing. Tricks of the light. There was nobody lurking down in the frozen tomb of B1.

Flora waited by the entry as the guttering lamp and I picked our way back toward her across the rag piles. She was twisting the bottle dejectedly in her hands.

'I've been thinking, Daddy.'

– *uh ok* –

'I want to go to the Family.'

She no longer looked anything like Mai, especially not the hungry laughing Mai I'd just run from. Very small and scared.

'I want them to take care of us.'

'That's not possible, baby. I'm sorry. All we have is each other.'

Flora nodded, not looking me in the eye. What had she expected?

'Let's take some blankets, huh? That'll cheer you up. We'll be nice and toasty tonight.'

'But what if animals smell them? Smell them and find us?'

Shit. That was a good point.

'That won't happen, sweetheart. I promise.'

But it did. And it was Flora who spotted it.

'Daddy!'

She clutched my arm, voice husking.

'Daddy, something's following us.'

—*oh god*—

I looked away for a moment, composing myself.

'What did it look like?'

Hungry, even given what we'd witnessed, to see an animal.

'A shadow. Low to the ground. Like a reflection. I only saw it for a second.'

'Right.'

No amount of big strong man pee was going to put this stalker off. It had happily spread an entire settlement around the insides of their home like paint. Hauling the incriminating blankets out of the sled, not giving myself time to think.

'You break sharp right. Go for one-thousand-avocado steps, then turn left. Go two-thousand-avocado, then tuck in behind those rocks. See them? Be sure to keep your head down.'

'What will you do?'

I cradled her woolly little face in my hands.

'If you're my brave girl and do exactly as I tell you, Daddy will be safe. Go on, now. Step as light as you can.'

Shouldn't be too hard, a feather would make more impression on the landscape. I hoped I hadn't just said my last words to my daughter. It'd be typical for me to be caught in a big fat lie.

Continuing on what had been our heading, I dragged the blankets along the ground behind the sled. Get a nice big smell trail going. Nice to find that in all the excitement counting still came automatically, although I'd not practiced since the days of Flora's seizures. If I missed an avocado and we got separated we might not find one another. Only abandoning my girl, my greatest fear. No stress.

When I guessed far enough I ditched the blankets, already mourning the comfort they'd promised. The folk from the car park had really known how to weave.

Now for the hard part. I hoisted the sled in my arms, already hating this plan. Walked back half a dozen awkward, wobbling backward steps in my previous footprints. It felt like the sinews in my arms were letting go.

Before the limbs sheared right off I quickly hot-footed it to where Flora was hiding. Had a bad moment rounding the rocks, stupid imagination; she was right where she should be. My good girl.

Disciplined, Flora didn't let out a squeak on seeing me appear puffing and gasping to let the sled down. Her eyes shone. I would've been overjoyed as well, but I think I popped a hernia.

We fled as fast and as far as we could. As often as I could stand I carried the sled for a clutch of staggering steps. And when we found snow we scrubbed everything down including our skinny shivering selves.

It seemed to work. Insofar as nothing butchered us that day beneath the indifferent clouds. Nor the next. I still think of that shadow, that hidden predator back there. Tearing up the blankets with our scent in its snout. Still restlessly searching for us. We were just another animal to it.

FLORA & JIM

Chapter Four

Migration

My croaked, 'What are we going to do?' sounded feeble. Decades-ago-me would've rolled his eyes, but I'd done my dash for today. Hard to believe I'd once been a young buck, junking along despair's shore, thinking myself clever.

—*your logic's no good, jimbo*—

Plenty no good. If I succumbed to wretchedness, so would Flora. Nothing to do then but plant our weary backsides in the dust, wait for entropy to plug the sun. I struggled to straighten my spine, find that carefree smirk that asserted, '*See honey, Daddy was only funning.*'

For all my efforts, depression was a page stuck to my forehead.

'Dad-dee!' Flora chided. 'Let's get after the terrible two before they pull too far ahead.'

That brightened me up. Terrible two. The other father was terrible.

Wiry as a burro, Flora took on most of the hauling. Standing there tapping her foot at me she was scarcely even puffed, though her exposed throat glowed a bright cherry red.

And she was right. The land sprawled at our backs was pinched to a husk. Teeth rattled in my head. Stick arms and legs felt alien when I patted myself down. I could hardly see how, but escape demanded a time of faith and miracles.

No more poor suburban homes to be dug out. Those were the days of scratching painfully at frost with chunks of steel; catch a nasty welt if you slipped. What homes were left lay too deep and calorie-expensive to excavate. Scant promise of anything, even bugs waiting inside.

I hadn't loved the routine of digging. It was hard, but also provided rhythm and purpose. Its loss left me adrift and disoriented. The only things that remained plentiful were mounds of frozen earth to trip over and break your toe.

They were scattered according to the layout of a long-ago grid, clear sign some bastard animal had been in to pip the goodies. Being better shovelers they tunnelled casually, easy as a trip to the shops.

Holes pocked the ground, placid black eyes staring up at the sun. Venture too close, and you might never come back. Humans were so much easier to open than cans.

That scene at the car park settlement still had me gasping my way out of strangling night terrors. Again I'd find myself unwrapping its gory secret from swaddles of dirty blanket. Tromping around on top of all that blood. Perhaps having seen it, some part of me would always be stranded there.

Poor Flora cried into her pillow, too, those first few nights. She's proven more resilient in the long term. Sometimes I rub my dry tired eyes, glance at my sleeping angel and wonder if she even remembers. I'd give a lot for a taste of that fortitude.

Worse, the sinking feeling in my shrivelled belly told me Mai was drawing close again. Haggard, and alert for the faintest flicker, I couldn't stop myself compulsively glancing behind. Anxiety burned calories I could ill afford to lose. Sharing restless energy with the animals, their grace, Mai'd found the suburbs more of a home than us. Perhaps she might stay if we left.

I held out hope Flora hadn't noticed. Told her I was nervous of animals, my little white lie. My daughter may have been smiling as she nodded and turned away; surely a mere quirk of hungry bones beneath tatty balaclava.

A woolly face that these days revealed the form of the adult developing beneath, rather than lumpenly sliding away. Her mother's inheritance was finally starting to fit. I liked it less and less.

All of this had transpired to push us outward until we fetched up on this vast artificial shelf. I suspected what we faced was a commercial dock, though the cranes were long gone. To approach water we had to negotiate a maze of shipping containers.

They'd once been stacked as high as mountains. Over time the poor sucker supporting others' ambitions from down below had inevitably collapsed, taking the whole stack down, scattering them in every direction.

Red-gold was already staining the tilting, leaning nightmare by the time we shuffled in. I refused to even consider tackling it without a full day of light on our side. Some structures still played at being solid but this was obviously, ludicrously unsafe.

No greater prospect of security to push left or right for a week trying to get around it. Without much deliberation we selected a cube to shelter from the dark hours in, probably once the site office.

Spirits dropped the moment we stepped inside. Rustic, even by abandoned crapshack standards. With the door clanged shut it was midnight already.

I wasn't even game to make a fire. It didn't look like there was anything for us and I was tired, bone weary. My joints were sobbing. I just wanted to lie down and go away.

'We have to have food, Daddy.'

'There isn't enough to burn,' I groused, trying to put her off. I wasn't a leggy adolescent with a body struggling to blossom and grow, hadn't been yanking the sled all day. I wasn't hungry.

—lies—

I *was* hungry, of course I was. My stomach a miserable shrivelled thing suckling on my spine.

'We have to at least try.'

Her tone softened.

'There'll be something, Daddy. Like you always say; life clings on in pockets and corners. The cold isn't the end. We just have to look.'

Oh God, had I ever been so embarrassingly naïve? Sounded like something off the back of a chip packet. Nonetheless, duty called, so I wearily stirred stiff limbs to do it all again. For her. A calming ritual of stacking and lighting.

'Crack the door a little, honey. Let the smoke out.'

The walls seemed leaky enough but I was no longer a man to take chances.

I'd not been kidding about the fuel. We'd a few bits left; unless we turned up more kindling this might be our last go-around. At least we'd see some comfort out of the fire, and I *did* start to feel better. Warmed the shards out of chapped hands while we waited.

Heat slipped inside, made a little spot of hope. I'd have been a fool to freeze without using it—what good would that last bit in reserve have been, then?

Finally, against all odds, a stirring that did not come from either of us. I squinted. It wasn't a trick of the shadows. Flora practically bounced.

'Daddy, get ready!'

But what was it? Pinkish, inflamed and thick as your finger. A silent albino horde had crept outside and were wiggling their digits in at us from all over. Only these fingers kept on coming, impossibly, more and more of their length slumping through to drop to the floor. Only the absurdity kept me from screaming. The larger part of my brain was convinced it wasn't happening.

A kind of worm came out of the walls. Blind, coiling. Difficult to pick up. I'd have done anything to not have to eat them. Not have that wet gleaming jelly in my gut.

Cooking hardly helped. They lashed about when applied to hot tin, seeking freedom, anything. Perhaps an explanation for this sudden agony when they'd emerged from hibernation simply wanting life. All I could offer was a nauseated groan.

'Sorry. I'm sorry. I want to live. I want her to live.'

'What's that, Daddy?'

'Nothing, sweetie. Just Daddy being silly again.'

I couldn't watch the gusto with which Flora stuffed worms in her expressionless face.

As badly as every cell of me moaned for sleep, I spent that night constantly jerking to high alert. Plagued by visions of a gruesome last Johnny-come-lately round of worms, lured out from the walls by my rank sweat.

Worms tapping and searching their way closer to my helpless comatose body once I'd shut my eyes. Leaving a web of unclean slime on everything they touched. And Flora, balaclava rucked up over her high gleaming forehead in the dark. Come slithering silently across my blankets to cram worms into her frozen maw.

Every time I sat up the night was bland and innocent. No matter how hard I stared or listened. The wind sizzled outside, my daughter snug in her own cocoon. As it turned out, waiting pointlessly through the long night hours was what being an old man was all about. Waiting for calamity to drop on our heads.

Which made for a crotchety start the next morning. It was almost too cold to get going. Night pooled and lingered, a gnawing chill that encouraged limbs to slow, blood to settle into icy mush.

There wasn't enough space inside the cramped box for the prickly distance I needed. Trudging out I turned back to glare at the site office, waiting for Flora to emerge so we could get on with it. I caught my breath.

What had been a perfunctory bunker when we laid ourselves down was now all over with white tentacles! Stark with the ashy dawn breaking behind it reared over me like some strange anemone caught in the act of exploding. Stranded here so near to the water we had yet to even glimpse.

My knees loosened. I won't lie, my bladder too. The world could transform overnight, leaving me that bit further up the beach from things I could cope with. I thought about running but my joints weren't up for it. I thought about slitting my wrists. Would it hurt?

Flora came tromping out and when she saw what I was gaping at she whooped for joy. A practical girl, not mired in outdated superstitious dread. Once I saw the phenomenon through her eyes I understood, too, and was a daft old man for losing my nerve.

Disturbed by our warmth the blind mindless worms had fled out as well as in, and the night wind got them. They'd been frozen as they emerged in a writhing halo around the building.

Flora insisted on circling the bunker to hack them all off, calling it bounty, calling it another few days of life. I sat to rest my wobbling legs and, thinking me still mired in my sulk, she worked alone.

I felt foolish, was all. The strangeness of that stark and sudden vision seemed scorched on the inside of my eyelids. I wanted to get my fingers in and scrape it away, demolish that moment of awe and almost religious dread.

Even with such an early start we burned the day to get perhaps ninety percent of the way through the container maze.

It was another world in there. Wind baffled into lethargy by sudden corners. Impossibly crisp blocks of shadow striped the ground, looking like if you stepped on one you'd plummet and vanish.

What shuffling sounds we made were reduced to flat claustrophobic murmurs. WE couldn't move briskly, and it was hard to keep warm. Flora and I marked our tedious progress with long scrapes of white concrete across the faded logos of long-extinct shipping companies.

Once upon a time they'd made fortunes flooding this port, and the cavernous city beyond, with more than the population would ever need. Exotic delicacies in gross abundance. A cut earmarked to get tossed before they even opened the wrapping.

For big steel boxes, many of the containers turned out to be a hell of a lot frailer than they looked. Only the corners seemed to have held up. In the middle your hand could unexpectedly punch through, setting off a restless clanging and freezing you in place, in a rain of cold sweat and rust. Staring at each other with wide eyes. Didn't dare move until it settled.

As the day of dead-ends and crossing dazzling light to shadow wore on, we needed to be careful. Far more careful than fatigue inclined us. Who was I kidding, I *started* tired. The perfect recipe for disaster.

Flora was on ahead, curiosity had her by the nose. I limped along passively. I saw her bend toward something on the ground. And still my numb instincts mumbled, *it's fine*.

A sullen mutter was our only warning. It might even have come from me. Three stories of metal container slumped. They had glanced down at the trespassing human bugs and wanted us squished.

I saw the blocks come over me as though they were flying, coming down from the sky. Inky shadows raced across the ground and swallowed me up. All my thoughts went white like drifting snow. My mind was trying to make it not hurt.

Fortunately, old reliable didn't need superfluous input. My rickety body threw itself gracelessly back while I was stupidly mulling was this really happening.

I sprawled, and all the adrenaline in the world belatedly dumped into my bloodstream. Didn't make me any braver. I cowered and hung onto the earth, cold and sick with the shakes.

On all sides great curls and panels of metal crashed, rocked to rest in their new configuration. A giant's wind chimes had been hurled to the floor. The sound alone battered me senseless.

Gradually things quietened down.

I finally found the courage to raise my ringing head, baffled I'd somehow not been smashed into jelly.

'Daddy?'

—*oh thank god*—

I hadn't been deafened, either.

'Flora? Flora!'

'Daddy are you ok?'

Was I? You know, forget the facts, she already sounded terrified.

'I'm fine sweetie. Bit of a fright.'

'Daddy I'm so sorry—I thought there was some paper and I went poking to get it, I didn't think. Daddy, I almost *killed* you …'

My good girl, trying to make our next fire a sure thing.

'Flora, I'm coming!'

Now I had something to do with all that adrenaline. I wobbled upright. I was vibrating so hard my teeth almost cracked.

'Stay where you are! He might've set more traps!'

'What?' she yelled back, confused.

I was already eeling my way into the fresh mess toward her. My Flora. Unharmed, oh thank God.

'That fucker Alfred did this. Set a trap for us, I just know it! No random scrap of paper would've survived out in the open this long …'

'Daddy, no.'

'… knew you'd be curious about some damn paper …'

'Daddy, Charlie wouldn't *do* that! Why do you always think that way? Nobody set any traps! Look around. It's all just … just really old and crap. Like everything!'

—*like everything. like me?*—

She was sharp, impatient with me and my shocked rambling. No doubt she'd had a fright, too. Something of my chagrin must have communicated. Flora relented.

'We're both tired, Daddy.'

I cleared my throat, dismayed by how readily tears welled. My nerves were shot.

'So where's this infamous paper, then?'

A flush stippled up into her balaclava. Furnace under that woollen face. I wanted to warm my hands by it; maybe my head did take a knock.

'I ... lost it. Under the collapse. I'm sorry Daddy.'

Suddenly, insufferably weary. What did we have to show?

'Never mind, sweetheart.'

'Maybe there's more on the other side? Let's go see.'

'No way. We'll go tomorrow.'

'But Dad-dee, we're almost there!'

'I've had enough for today. Traps or not, Alfred won't get too far ahead.'

The sea could be treacherous, the literature claimed. Oh, I hoped so. My secret desire was that given time, the other father and the boy would die out there. Then our task would merely be dragging the bodies back to shore, one for each.

Another night at the site office to see us safely through didn't seem too much to ask. Flora could have argued, citing low food, low fuel, low spirits. Her kindness in letting it slide indicated what shape I must be in better than any mirror.

Trying not to seem too obvious I laid my bed in a different spot for the night. Perhaps sleep would be waiting for me here.

Flora cocked her head curiously.

'Why are you so far away, Daddy?'

—*think fast, jimbo*—

I fanned the air, trying to make light.

'Well sweetie, Daddy's a bit tootie tonight.'

Wasn't far from the truth. The worms sat uneasily in my belly. I'd witnessed them cooked: definitely dead, yet still my guts squirmed.

Flora stared expressionlessly for so long I began to feel

nervous. Finally I recognised the faint tightening around her eyes. A smile.

'Maybe that's what happened with the boxes today?'

I was surprised into a chuckle.

'One good pop, and I was almost Jim jam.'

We only had the flickering lamp, which was miserable. The walls didn't keep heat too well. Enough to keep us defrosted, which I guess was better than nothing.

Wanting to conserve her strength Flora rolled straight into sleep. I was reminded of folktales, where excited children close their eyes to make Santa come sooner. Down the chimney to deliver presents. Every day a gift.

I scrunched up my face in turn, did my best. Obviously I was just too far from the good little boy I'd once been. No Saint Nick for me. No sleep. I was still dry-eyed and staring when the tapping began.

From outside, where nothing was supposed to live. Only faintly discernible above the wind. Soft, but insistent. A polite request for entry. The tapping roamed right the way around the office, and settled on a point closest to where I lay trying not to breathe.

Trying to hide, to trick it, would never work. I was known. In the precise way I in turn knew the better father; bitter with hatred and longing; and would never let him go.

No wall in the world would deny Mai should she want in. No, she was knocking so as not to disturb our sleeping daughter. She was knocking to scare me.

And it was working. Dread pulled me in two different directions: of Mai coming in. Of Flora then waking up and seeing her …

As quietly as I could, I crept from the comforting blue bubble of the pond. Crept to the wall, where worms had come coiling through.

'Go away,' I pleaded, already shaking from the cold.

But of course she wouldn't. Mai hated being alone.

Was that a voice? I thought the wind sighed, '*Flora.*'

'Everything,' I hissed. 'I've done *everything* for her. But you—you let me down first, Mai. You lied. You lied to both of us. If you hadn't lied we could have gone back. Why ..?'

Snot was running. I smeared it impatiently, wanting some answer, an explanation for my wife's betrayal.

'Why would you do that? Our future ... our family was going to be so beautiful. All the signs said so. You ruined it.'

Tap, tap, tap.

I could almost hear the mockery. Dreamy-eyed Jim and his faith in signs and omens. I bitterly regretted confessing my nervous superstitious nature to Mai, although once upon a time withholding any corner of my mind would have been stark sacrilege.

Laugh as much as she liked, the signs had always been there. Even when we were at our most desperate.

We'd been starving. My little family, all our plans, come to this.

The three of us huddled in an old brick outhouse shell and I had started a fire because Flora was right, you don't ever give up. Especially not with your hollow-eyed wife and baby depending on you.

We lit, and chafed our hands, and we waited with Flora's tiny swaddle pressed between our bodies. Shielding her from the world with what we had left. And Mai cried, raw wracking barks, her life come in a brutal circle.

I thought nothing would hatch. Was already nodding off, my wife's breath against my cheek. Wish I could say it was sweet as a thousand summers, which I guess was only true in my foolish heart.

But then the tiniest flicker caught my eye. Iridescent blue. So deep and rich it was almost a flower. I reached up and caught the fragment disbelievingly, gently between my hands.

We had woken a single, impossible butterfly. Stirred from hibernation to a world that no longer needed pollinators.

Seemingly content in the cave of my warm palms it fanned its wings, drying them. Where will you fly to, little thing? Beyond my grasp where is there for you to go?

The beauty hurt, but in a good way, like a shard of happiness driven through my sternum. This was life. This was how the sky used to be.

'Honey. Honey, look.'

Bursting with wonder I turned carefully to show Mai. Terrified the fragile thing I held would shatter before she got to see. My smile felt fit to split my face. Suddenly, I just knew we were going to be ok.

'Look at …'

Mai snatched the butterfly from my hands and popped it in her mouth. She chewed while staring at me defiantly. Then bent to kiss the fragment of mush into Flora's tiny mouth. Gleaming flecks of blue scale on the faces of both mother and daughter.

'There's your damned sign.'

Mai whispered so as not to disturb the baby, but never before had a whisper contained such depths of malice.

Crammed into a brick shitter at what I assumed was the end, I had wanted that tiny enchanting thing to be something, or mean something. I wanted Mai to look at it and understand how much I loved her.

Instead I pulsed with humiliation and fury.

—*jim! something's got …*—

I gave a muffled scream and flinched back from the wall.

Outside, the taps trailed as though Mai was casually walking away. Dragging her fingers along the wall as she went.

Tap ... tap ... gone.

All in gooseflesh with my teeth clattering, returning to the pond I thought I caught a raised silhouette within. Sitting up watching me. The gleam of cold judgmental eyes.

When I pulled aside the duck sheet Flora was fast asleep. Just my conscience plaguing me. I wrapped myself snugly, limbs drawn close to try and get warm.

Just before I went under, my conscience whispered.

'Sh, Daddy. I won't let her get you.'

The next day our blazed path was mercifully simple to follow. The new container fall already looked like it'd been there forever.

—nothing to see here, move along folks—

I did move along, stepping past quickly. This was a place where we'd nearly lost out. It reeked of bad luck, I couldn't wait to be shot of it.

From the shadowy maze we emerged back out into daylight, blinking even behind goggles. Not especially bright, just searing compared to where we'd been. We were at the port's artificial shore.

Every poem described the sea as restless, unfathomable. Centuries of human anguish and longing. Yet here the water lay beneath a glowering sky. Frozen. As motionless and pointless as the rest of the world.

I marvelled at the amount of liquid water there'd once been here. Now my skin cracked and fissured so deeply, I felt I could shed it right here on the dock and be revealed another creature entirely.

Perhaps if you went far enough there'd be rocking waves, the cradle of living things. Seagoing plants, even. Something had to be making the air we breathed. Potentially a life to be made, but I'd read all the wrong books. Nothing I could grasp. With the skills at my disposal I looked out and all I saw was extinction.

I didn't like the cast of those clouds, either. Clouds over water were foreign, I couldn't understand them, but they *looked* clannish, huddling up like that. Curiously, way out on the horizon, giants seemed to be crowding out of the frozen surface to touch those clouds.

Broken giants? The light was such I couldn't discern what or how far away they were. Reluctant to reveal the extent of my impairment by asking Flora. I didn't even know if it was a true sea we faced. A bay? A lake?

I had no map, but footprints led out so I had to cinch my belt and trust my counterpart did. That the obstacle could be crossed. Surely he'd never in a million years lead his little boy out there otherwise, no matter how pressed. Not Alfred. Nothing was too good for *his* child.

'Daddy, look at this.'

Flora was on hands and knees at the edge where concrete met solid ice. Wiping frost and gravel away to peer through. Risking her paws, doing that. Better to use some kind of tool.

'Can we eat it?'

Her default query for anything new.

Creaking, I struggled down onto my own knee to look. Deep water here, for ships. Invited vertigo. I blinked a couple of times, thinking I was seeing a vortex of butterflies, but of course that was nostalgic nonsense.

An impressive array of trash mingled down there. So perfectly frozen into clear ice it looked set in Perspex. I'd never really seen the packaging colours so sharp before. Thought I recognised a couple of logos.

They must've all looked like this back in the day. Machined to be irresistible. Consumers couldn't help themselves, not even when discarded packets heaped up in bright mountains and clogged the waterways.

—*ooh, these'll last a thousand years!*—

Thanks, assholes. Hope your candy was nice.

Pollutants also bloomed amid the motionless tornado. Rank blobs of sickly chemical from the port, maybe, or the suburbs. Or perhaps sickness had leeched from the people themselves.

'No honey. It's pretty, but I don't think we could eat any of that.'

Flora immediately lost interest. I could have wandered back and forth marvelling for a bit longer, but fancy colours didn't change the fact that there was nothing useful on this shore.

The heavy horizon with its strange giants beckoned, *yes, come on, come on my dear*. And without warning Flora stepped out onto the ice, in that awkward teen manner of lunging rather than walking. The sled clunked after her.

'Flora? Flora!'

Why was I shouting? Except this felt wrong, nothing ever felt right. I ought to be out in front in case it was dangerous.

'Flora!'

Not that shouting did any good. Flora wasn't to be daunted, with her fearless comic strides into the future. My only choice was to copy the sled and skitter in her wake.

If not for sheets of grit blown out from the shore the slippery surface would've been impassable. Our traction was the residue of crumbling buildings and the crumbled lives of those who came before. A seemingly limitless supply, although I knew in my boots that couldn't be true. "Endless" was what they had thought when everything was theirs; now here they were, gritting my feet.

The sky seemed to bleed a nervous, twitching energy. Pregnant with anger, the foreign clouds waited out the hours as we tramped our way into their embrace. Waited until we had irrevocably renounced land. Committed ourselves.

Then the wind kicked up all at once. The clouds dropped their bellies right onto the ice, bunching into looming frowns. *Silly humans. You go splat now.*

Still Flora pushed on. We were struggling into the cold wind. I kept one hand on the sled, terrified I might be torn off and flung into the sky. The scarred and sun-bleached sled had looked translucent moments ago but now glowed bubble-gum pink beneath my hands, fresh as the day it was cast. The colours were too vivid. We were all bits of trash, fighting not to be churned.

Flora must have known there was more to the abnormal storm front than I, and she'd squared her jaw and led us into the teeth of it regardless.

—*be brave, daddy*—

My eyes weren't up to scratch; once we got within range, nothing wrong with my nose. The wind was slapping straight into our faces bringing the bad news.

Carnivore stench. Squinting as hard as I could revealed a great indistinct mass was being driven before the storm, herded across the ice. Coming to sweep us up.

'Flora!'

Flying grit filled my mouth. Had to spit into my sleeve. I struggled but I'd never catch her, never stop her. I couldn't even overtake the sled.

My daughter *did* respond, although it floored me to identify the sound drifting back. It came and went with the shrilling wind, undercut by the rasp-rasp of sled on uncertain surface.

Flora was laughing. Cackling at her skidding steps, the way she slid when unready. Laughing defiantly in the face of what was coming for us.

This, I realised incredulously, was so terrifying it was funny. Broke your brain; snapped that little cut-off switch for "too much" right off.

Flora's mania lent courage. There was a storm coming in, a mass migration of deadly animals, and my wild reckless daughter was laughing. So was I, taking shuffling run-ups to a tentative gliding step.

'They're going to eat us!' I cried, and even that tickled my funny bone. Brain definitely broken.

'Up ahead!' Flora called back over her shoulder. 'Those are ships up ahead. We have to make it!'

Before the storm breaks over us. Before the animals reach us. I tried to push being overwhelmed by a horde of shaggy locusts out of my mind, the both of us stripped to bone an arm's reach from safety. The wind would scatter what's left.

The first ship we reached; clearly a ship and not a giant, though it was massive enough; was mostly buried at a steep angle. Not that we had time to be picky. The furthest vessel from us was already shuddering under assault.

I didn't more than glance at the fuzzy blur of the oncoming beasts, trying to preserve what little sanity I had left, tucked away with the shreds of my principles. At least the ship's extreme angle let us reach the rail. All aboard.

'Get up,' I gasped, grasping for nautical terms. Never studied boats. 'Onto the … poop deck.'

Now Flora was laughing so hard she was nearly bent double. We were hysterical. So overwhelmed we'd gone hysterical.

'You first, poopy! I've gotta lift the sled up.'

With obliteration rolling in we struggled off the ice singing, '*Poop deck, poop deck.*' Staggering about like we were drunk. The angry wind wanting to fling us back down to be devoured.

The ship clanged as numerous great weights leaped aboard. Standing jumps up from the ice.

—*onto the poop deck*—

A hatch was open and we stumbled through dragging the sled like a parachutist his chute. Slammed the door.

Curious noses hit the other side, snuffling after a pair of squishy snacks. Us snacks sat on our side in the dimness with hands clamped hard across our mouths to keep inappropriate giggles from spurting out.

FLORA & JIM

Chapter Five

Postcards from Fauna

We heard the wind. Whoo, getting shriller. It was losing its temper.

The floor juddered as great feet knocked about on the other side. Hooves? Claws? Enough to make deck plates boom. Enough to see you instinctively bunch up inside yourself, becoming small. Not wanting to be noticed.

Humour was shut off like a current, as snuffling began low down by the door. Flora and I stared at each other, as much as we could see, goggle-eyed.

I don't know how my daughter felt but every hair of mine stood on end. The investigation was wet, grunting, congested. It delivered puffs of sour meaty breath into our refuge.

Another grunt, then an excited bleat. Loud. So loud we clapped our hands over our ears, hearts seizing.

Run, my nerves insisted and legs quivered trying to obey.

Shh, whispered my brain in reply, fat lot of good it had ever done. *Be still. Be silent. You don't exist.*

I don't think we were fooling them. With a shushing sound a long tongue curled through the gap beneath the door. Literally uncurled from its tight nautilus spiral, like a honeyeater's tongue, to wave about questioningly. Were we the honey?

All along its length resembled the skin of a cactus, edged with toothy little spines sticking every which way. A tongue for pulling prey screaming from their hidey-holes.

Fumbling about, the tongue ventured too close to Flora's boot. Grey curdled saliva hung off it in strings, never quite falling. She jerked her foot away with a muted squeak of revulsion.

Not muted enough. More tongues joined the party, poking and exploring our space. Barely able to see what was reaching for us we had to dance and contort in silent pantomime terror to avoid them. Alerted mainly by the splat of saliva against walls as they became more riled out there.

Bumping, massively, and squealing. Working themselves into frenzy: Hey you guys, this food's trying to get way, this food is *fun*! To get at the tiny gap they must be pressed flank to steaming flank out there.

We wanted to creep further into the ship to move away, didn't dare without more light. And we couldn't spark up with those maniacs outside. They'd take the door apart.

Which they were working themselves up to anyway without our help. I ought to have risked it.

Flora didn't duck quite fast enough and a tongue glanced across her shoulder. The teeth stuck fast in her sleeve, yanking her violently toward the door like a rag doll.

'Dad-dee!' she hissed.

She'd be plunged straight into that seething nest of other tongues. I braced my back against the wall and kicked out with both boots, trying to wallop it off her.

—*oh no you don't! not my girl!*—

One beast outside was really shrilling now, knowing it had something on the line. Tongues flew about. Hooves/claws flailed. The door cracked and groaned. That's it, they're coming in.

I steeled myself to be ready. Hyperventilating, shaking sweat out of my eyes. I'd never be ready.

I'd thought the storm was already on us. Now it really hit. The light coming beneath the door dimmed abruptly, somebody turning down the sun. *Whooo* became a garbled roar, clotted with chips of ice.

Squeals gave way to pained yelps. Whatever they may be, the animals were smart enough to decide the exposed "poop deck" was no longer a fun spot. Scurrying and urgent grunts as they dropped off the ship.

All except for the one that held Flora hostage. Its tongue was hooked and it couldn't let go.

She was flung around and battered mercilessly against the door as it tried to suck the appendage through the gap where any little girl, no matter how skinny, clearly wouldn't fit. BANG-BANG-BANG. Mindlessly.

Flora stoically bit down on the pain, refusing to make a noise. I hammered with my boots again and again, futilely. Then she slipped free of her jacket, having managed to undo the fastenings while being tossed about.

The tongue and its prize whipped away beneath the door. We listened to the final animal scramble away, whimpering piteously, making for the protected lee of the ship.

Was it over? We both sat breathing heavily in the dark.

'Honey … are you ok?'

No one should have to wait so long for an answer. Then Flora's voice came, a bit out of puff.

'My jacket!'

She sounded pissed off.

Now I dared shuck my balaclava with shaking hands, slapping it against my leg to let grit out. Against my face the darkness felt solid, lifeless. Immediately apparent how much colder the storm made things.

'The lamp …'

'Already on it.'

My good girl. The besieged door failed to entirely bar the gusts now that the wind had its dander up. Our little flame wavered wildly in Flora's hands. I all but snatched it from her in my eagerness to be rid of the dark.

Our pursuers had wasted their opportunity in probing, playing. Now to see what we'd gained by their loss. We crowded a narrow space, like a coffin built for two. That wasn't me being morbid. Just the feeling I got setting foot in any structure these days.

The sled abutted the door—my clever Flora again!—in case that might've held the beasts a second longer. Metal steps ahead, from the look of it. No place to go but down.

The steep canted angle of the eternally sinking ship made me vaguely queasy. With no line of reference the world was out of true; I very much wished to see the horizon to straighten myself. But with the animals, the storm, fat chance.

Puffs of frost through the door caressed my cheek. If

anything, the long dim exhale from down those steps was even worse. I took a deep breath of my own, wiggling the headgear back on before my nostrils froze off.

'Out of the frying pan, hey?'

Flora didn't hear. I'd forgotten to raise my voice to compete with the wind. She had her back to me, examining the wall with fascinated fingertips. I watched her hands rove, pulling threads and fibres from the gloves. A hatch work of scratches, through the paint and into metal. No. A drawing.

Had to flatten myself against the far side to take it in. A heavy horizontal line, the frozen sea outside. Nice and desolate. And a figure in the distance, looking back over its shoulder at us.

'Honey, stop touching that.'

'Why?'

'It's eerie, that's why. And you're ruining your gloves.'

'What is it?'

'Just an artwork. Maybe a goodbye message, somebody working up the courage to leave.'

As likely an explanation as any. It had been scratched painstakingly over time, with a pin or nail. Lines over obsessive lines. Somebody had something sharp. Best remember that, in case they were still around.

'Is that what people do? Say goodbye.'

'Well, in various ways I guess. People want to be remembered.'

Flora took a sharper look down the stairs.

'So someone lived here. Bad news for us.'

True. Unless they croaked unexpectedly, occupants generally meant nothing good would be left.

'We're not likely to find out standing here.'

I was itchy to move on. Didn't like how with the shifting illumination the figure in the distance seemed to stutter and jerk. Like it was considering turning around. Coming back to see who'd been sleeping in its bed. A goodbye message, indeed.

Good riddance to you.

'Let's get you warmed up first, though.'

I bundled Flora in my own too-big coat, a cave of my body heat.

'How's your shoulder?'

'Just sore. From when it rattled me. I'd like to give the same back.'

In lieu of an overcoat I swathed myself in one of the tarps from the sled. Wasn't ideal, or quiet for moving around in. Flora was massaging her shoulder and I gave her a crackly salute.

'Welcome aboard the S.S. Flora, ma'am.'

'Dad-dee! Quit being silly.'

That wasn't what her tone said. Never stop being silly, Daddy. Never stop making it ok.

The banshee wind diminished as we followed the stairs down. We had to brace awkwardly against the wall to account for the ship's funhouse tilt. I ticked them off: strained neck, wrenched spine, for the love of God the knees.

—*not as bad as flora, though*—

Moments ago she was being whipped about. Didn't see her grousing, though she moved as stiffly as her old Dad.

Our narrow rat tunnel soon opened up into a warehouse-like space. We stepped onto a floor of solid ice that represented true level, both of us stumbling awkwardly as we made the transition. Little wisps of fog curled from its surface.

From here on in the ship was submerged and frozen under. So this was the end of the line. I couldn't get past the blurred impression of some kind of mass down there, in the ice. Although I got right down on my knees to peer through the greeny-grey it was too dark.

'Check every corner, honey. It's going to be night soon. We need fire or we'll freeze our ta-tas off in here.'

Not the whole story. I needed to see what was under our feet. We found scant traces of the past resident. Mainly where they'd hammered futilely at the ice trying to get at whatever was down there. Our artist locked in here, going stir-crazy.

Occasionally the ship's sides would boom as the wind clobbered it. We were sheltered from the worst down here. As we searched and found nothing it became sinkingly clear this was where we'd be spending the night. The day darkened in the grip of the storm. Flora's mood plummeted, as it so often did.

I missed the early warning signs. Put them down to her shoulder giving her grief, which it quite rightly should. The whole arm might have been pulled off like a chicken wing from one of my cookery books. Flora's question came abruptly after a space of dangerous silence.

'Do you think they made it across?'

'Hmm?'

I looked up from my pensive study of the ice.

'Charlie and Alfred. Do you think they're ok? Or did the tongues ..?'

I guess it was normal to feel upset, given the time we'd spent chasing them. In fact, the other father and his son, the pursuit, must be the only constant in Flora's young life. If you subtracted me.

Horrible, in that light, to suppose animals might nab them first. Tear those bags apart with barbed tongues and eat everything.

'Oh honey. That's what you've been worrying about? After all these years, you know it's not their luck. I'm sure they made it.'

She rounded on me. We hadn't even lit the fire yet and there were flames in Flora's eyes.

'What will you ask?'

'Baby …'

'What happens when we catch them?'

I held my hands out helplessly.

'Sweetheart, what do you want to hear?'

'Tell me why we never went back to The First Family, no matter how hungry we got. We wouldn't be chasing Charlie if we did!'

The accusation sucked the breath out of me. This was a new Flora. One who knew things without being told. Secrets behind that stone wall of a face. Canny and patient, this person. I was afraid if I lied to her, she'd know.

'Honey … we left the Family 'cause we wanted a baby. We wanted you. And babies were the one thing that wasn't allowed.'

I was supposed to be helping Uncle Ebo in the kitchen. I'd been unsettled and twitchy all morning, ultimately resulting in being downgraded to observer-only for having "ants in my pants".

I knew why I was really sent to the other side of the bench. It didn't have anything to do with damn ants.

Using the can opener had been a sort of treat. I liked its bold orange plastic, the efficient crunch-crunch as I turned the handle. Cracks zigzagged the grip and I had to be inordinately careful not to make things worse for the venerable old tool.

Only this time as the can's metal cracked upward, a putrid stink steamed out.

'Phew!'

Uncle Ebo caught a whiff from where he was standing.

'Don't remember calling for a tin of old dead feet. Luck of the draw, I guess; bound to get a few bad eggs. Just toss it in the bin, Jimbo.'

'Pity the bad egg is always me,' I muttered, reaching for another can from the stack.

Uncle Ebo smiled. He had an epic nose which Mai called alarming, but when he got that grin out it was pure honey drawing the flies in.

'Abena doesn't think you're bad. She never gave her own two boys a single smile more than she's handed you, and she adored those hellions more'n her hands and feet.'

'... maybe if she'd been nicer they'd still be around ...'

'What did you just say, boy?'

Never let it be claimed Ebo couldn't be wrathful. It was the only time he resembled his sister.

'... nothing ...'

'Now, Jimbo, I'm going to tell you this once. After that, I'm going to assume you've the basic brains to never smart off like that again.'

'Yes sir.'

I wasn't stupid. Smiles aside, if I crossed his sister Ebo was likely to stuff me in a can and nail it shut. It was nice when he treated me as a grown man, but not like this. Even my big self-absorbed head knew I'd taken a step too far.

'Long before she came to lead the Family, Abena lived in a cute little apartment with her husband and two boys. I couldn't have been prouder of those kids if they'd been mine and I guess Fury was ok, too, in his own way.'

'Aunt Abena's husband was named Fury?'

Actually, that made a lot of sense.

'Might not've been what he was born with, but "Fury" was how I met him and Abena had eyes as big as the moon already so I knew not to snigger. Anyways, I came over to check on them one day. I'd improvised a sort of pie I wanted to show off and growing boys need their food.

'So peaceful and quiet in the corridor. Straight away that wasn't right; they'd the run of the building, hell, the block; you could always hear those boys laughing, or humming, clicking, whistling, you name it. Regular cheeky cacophony, that apartment.

'But not this time. Unnaturally quiet, that's what I remember thinking. Nobody answered when I knocked but my hackles were up, so I pushed the door open.

'There was Abena sitting in that apartment that'd always seemed too small, but was now cavernous. Cold and alone, staring at the wall. She hadn't even bothered to light a fire. Heaven knows how long she sat there.

"Where are they, Abbee? Where are the boys?' I tried shaking her, yelling, got nothing and all the while going out of my mind. The simple truth was that at night her sons had started fussing. Hadn't been sleeping well. Claimed they were hearing something outside the window which was impossible twelve stories up. The apartment had been picked for defensibility.

'So they were all ragged from the boys' nightmares. One night Fury kissed her arm, said he'd check on them. Abena dropped back off, but when she woke again her husband and sons had vanished. No explanation. Couldn't have gotten past her to the door. She was exhausted, but no-one's that light a sleeper.

'She said she should have been the one to check on them. Fury was fine for a name, but Abena was best equipped to handle problems. I wasn't going to go arguing with her in such a state, but the basic fact is you can't be watching all the time. You just can't.

'I told her she couldn't stay there. Too many memories souring into ghosts. I insisted we pack and strike out, find other people, us no spring chickens and all. All she wanted to do was wait in that apartment to be reunited, one way or another.'

That didn't sound like the Aunt Abena I knew, none of it did. I hadn't yet learned that what you see of people, even those you've known years, is just a scratch on the surface.

'We had to do something. Luckily I can make myself a real burr up the ass when needs be. When all she wanted was to lie down, it was Abena who found and saved the Family.'

'Uncle Ebo ... did you ever want a family of your own?'

Ebo tipped his head back and roared laughter at that, dispelling the reflection of Aunt Abena's sadness, which was why I asked. I was tired of feeling like an asshole.

'Oh sure, just drowning in handsome options here! Let's see, it'd have to be that bitter old coot Isaiah. This may be the end of the world, but don't think for a second my standards have dropped that low.'

Interrupting the banter I snatched my hands back from the bench in disgust.

'Ugh!'

The second can opened. That same rotten smell.

Pinching my nose I peeked inside. Red pox across the can's interior, oozing rust. An indistinct black mass slopping about the bottom. Black wasn't a colour for food. My eyes widened: was it moving? *Slithering*?

'Let me see that.'

Frowning, Uncle Ebo took it from me. I was never so glad to relinquish anything in all my life.

'That's strange. They weren't swollen up. The seal looked good.'

He fished another can from mount ziggurat, gave the opener a half-dozen efficient cranks. Peered inside. I couldn't look.

'Ah, this one's fine. That's a relief. If more had gone rotten we'd be sending the scouts out again. Paisley would looove another chance to complain about her knees.'

Unbelievably, when he handed the opener back to me it happened again. The crack of metal I was coming to dread. The same soggy, dead-underpants whiff.

Uncle Ebo ran a hand over his smooth head, fretting.

'Jimbo, why don't you take a load off and just watch for a bit?'

Well, if ants in your pants was a thing, now I was practically dancing.

'But there's no such thing, right? You always say, 'Ah Jimbo and your omens,' and roll your eyes because it's just something from an old book, right?'

'Nothing personal little Jim, and no I don't believe in that mumbo-jumbo claptrap. Just ... being on the safe side, is all. It's not easy to find cans these days. Who knows how long these'll need to last.'

My dismay was interrupted by Mai who sidled through the door and grabbed my arm.

'Jim, can we have a word please? In *private*?'

When people growl at you through gritted teeth it's kind of hard to work out what they're saying. Uncle Ebo waved us off. He'd always been the nicest, but suddenly couldn't wait to see the back of me, off into the clutches of someone who growled.

'Don't have too much fun, you two.'

Mai bundled me into a closet. It wasn't lost on me that this was our special place, where we hid from chores. Where we'd been squirrelled away the first day I kissed her.

My heart gave a strained thump. I pursed my lips a bit in anticipation. I'd never seen her look more beautiful than now: somehow joyous, enraged, and terrified all at once.

'Jim, I'm pregnant.'

'Are you sure?'

Wrong thing to say, but I'd punched right out the other side of shock into a great unknown. Weirdly, the only coherent thought out here was of Aunt Paisley. Not her bad knees which, Uncle Ebo was right, she loooved to complain about. The way she sometimes dandled a little cocoon of blankets when she thought nobody was looking, and sang softly to herself. Pretending the world was kinder.

'Am I sure you stuck your dick in me and now my periods have stopped and my boobs feel full of concrete—yes Jim, I'm pretty fucking sure.'

I tried covertly studying to see if she showed, but Mai was already round. Where was the extra roundness supposed to go?

She slapped my hand.

'Stop looking at me like that!'

Fair.

'What are we going to do?'

Her eyes like distant, feverish stars.

'We can't stay. Your Family kooks, you know how they think, they'll never let us keep our baby. They'll put it out overnight or bury it in the waste pit or something. Their one big rule: no new babies. Old farts only for the old world.'

Aunt Paisley singing softly in a room by herself. Comforting a tiny absence. Comforting herself.

'I'm not sure they ...'

'We have to find my parents. My real family. Now.'

Certainty led the charge. Enough to kindle me, too, so long as I fanned it. Which I wasn't sure I wanted to.

'*Our* baby, Jim. And they *took me from my family*. Never forget that, they stole me! I know you've been protected from it but they're terrible people, they do terrible things.'

I didn't know what to think. My mind was wasting time spinning frantically, looking for a way out. Who could think straight with that rotten can stench still clogging their nostrils?

Was this the omen's warning? That our child was in danger?

'Look.'

Mai knew when her hooks were in, she took my hand.

'Stop panicking. I've been getting ready, a bit every day for years. And I've searched for my parents everywhere I can without arousing suspicion. That's everywhere nearby already checked.'

All this time, giddy in love, I'd thought Mai was happy here with me. That she'd settled down to build our new life.

'Hey.'

She took my face in her hands, looked deeply into my eyes. She'd been crying. How could I have missed that? But now a luminous smile lit up her face.

'It's going to be ok. My parents'll love you. You wanted a sign before you'd help me? Jim, we're going to have a baby.'

If you wanted a sign of change, a baby fit the bill alright. One you couldn't possibly ignore.

I was taken aback by the scope of supplies Mai had put together. My heart revived, at last, when I saw that it was enough for two. She had always planned on taking me with her. Wouldn't abandon the boy who'd faithfully left dinner outside her door.

That's when I knew I couldn't let her down.

Food, that was my role. I had to steal some food and meet Mai by the back door to make our escape. More heinous a crime than it seemed. There were less mouths to feed these days with old Aunt Aaliyah lost to the cold, wrapped for burial in a blanket of her own knitting, but also less to put in those mouths. The animals were becoming bolder.

The pantry, at the heart of the house, wasn't guarded though. That wasn't Uncle Ebo's way.

I knew I was wasting time standing staring into it. Mai would be getting fearful, might even leave without me. This was happening so fast. At least for me; not so much the patient spider my lover, now mother of my child, who'd been spinning this web most of her life. But looking at the shelves, all my labouring overheating mind could think of was the future.

A tomorrow for humanity the Family insisted didn't exist. Well, we were having a baby. There's mud in your eye. My hot blood was singing. A baby. A child deserved a future.

I went and got the wheelbarrow and I took everything. Every scrap of food. Tossing it angrily into the scoop with loud clangs.

I wasn't being careful like I promised Mai. Uncle Ebo found me while I was tying a tarp over the load. I looked up, and he was there. Watching silently. Sadness on his seamed face.

I thought about fleeing, just abandoning the wheelbarrow. The awful ashamed part of me spat and hissed from its corner, and proposed braining him with a can of beans. Bashing that weary sorrowful visage in so I wouldn't have to cope with it a second longer.

'Mai's pregnant,' I blurted. That being the only truth my brain would hold.

Ebo stepped closer and I worried he might seize me, or embrace me which would be worse, which would shatter me into a howling thing. So near, I couldn't help being aware of my slightness by comparison—not really a man, not yet. I was starting out. Not like Uncle Ebo with the weight of a whole life on top of him. He moved ponderously under the burden of everything he'd been, and done.

Ebo leaned past me into the looted pantry. I thought he was assessing the scope of my crime and tensed, every muscle. Ready for God knows what. He popped a board from the ceiling and retrieved something that had been hidden above it.

Eyes brimming, he handed it to me.

'What have you done?' Mai gasped when I appeared at the door with the overloaded wheelbarrow wobbling ahead of me. I shoved her forward roughly.

'Just go. Hurry.'

We feasted like pigs that night at our first camp. Gorged ourselves. I guess Mai was celebrating. I'd forgotten the can opener. Had to hammer tins open with a rock.

'The lamplight's so pretty,' Mai murmured dreamily as the blue tarp rattled. 'It's like our own peaceful little pond in here.'

I wondered if there was any room in her head for what consumed me. The thought of the Family gathering mournfully around the empty pantry. Sitting themselves stiffly on the floor to die.

I fixated on the orange can opener. In some way that cheery plastic blamed me, was testament to the selfish thing I'd done. How long did plastic last—a hundred years? The can opener would bear witness to guilt for a hundred years, long after I was dust. I couldn't even die and be free of it.

For the life of me, I never told Mai about the chocolate Uncle Ebo gave us to commemorate the birth of our child. Instead I snuck away while she was dozing. To squat in the chilling pre-dawn and force it all down, alone and all at once, as punishment.

Piece by hateful piece, sickly sweet. Until the disgust in my gut matched that of my head.

'Nothing mattered as much as you, baby. Nothing ever has.'

The information sank into Flora like a stone. What happened to it after that was invisible to me.

To endure the night we huddled in our pond, the outside draped in sheets, us fully clothed under more wraps. The lamp between us, so close we were nearly sitting on it. Wraiths of cold smoke writhed about our shanty, coming off the ice.

The longer we sat clattering our teeth, the more obvious it became this was not going to do. The chill radiation from the floor was too intense. It bit into my backside, gnawed knees and elbows.

We experimented with moving back up into the stairway, after a shred of comfort. Any gains were offset by the difficulty of wrapping the pond around us. The figure in the distance stared from its wall as we limped miserably down the stairs again.

Without kindling, I struggled fruitlessly to start a fire. My wits were becoming fuddled. Wasted a good share of the lamp mush. Our last chunks of poop-patty were too dense, wouldn't stay lit. Stupid past-me had been passing them over for fires for just that reason.

So desperate for warmth I strongly considered smothering skin in the gluey oil and setting myself alight.

'Daddy, stop squirming! You have to settle.'

'We're going to die if I can't get this fire going.'

Such was my depth of despair. I'd never outright stated "we're going to die" to my daughter before. Though it was on my mind a thousand times. No, I always smiled my fool smile, doolally honey, everything's going to be ok.

Flora lifted haunted eyes to mine.

—*oh, I've crushed her*—

I wanted to punch my big fat mouth. But that wasn't it.

From hidden pockets about her person Flora stiffly produced scraps of cereal box, packets, rags. Enough combustibles to save our lives. Enough to burn us to the waterline. All dense with tiny handwritten script.

Dumbfounded I held them like a handful of leaves.

'What are these?'

'Letters, Daddy. Letters from Charlie; only I call him Fauna. My Fauna.'

'Letters? Don't be ridiculous.'

'He's been leaving them for me. His Daddy doesn't know, either.'

The world seemed to slump. The void opened up beneath me by the halo of worms prised wider.

—*secret letters?*—

Love letters. There were so many of them.

'How long has this been going on?'

Now I sounded like a proper Dad. And Flora, a teen, properly defiant.

'Don't be upset.'

'Honey, you can't be his friend. You know that, right?'

'You had Mum. Why can't you let me have Fauna?'

'Because, sweetheart, one day we're going to catch them.'

I crumpled the missives in my fists. Flora's eyes widened as if I'd slapped her, but she didn't try to snatch her letters back.

How could I stand to read them? The scribblings of a young lad just as I'd been, fresh, innocent and yearning with all his heart towards someone. There was no way I could crouch here and bring each up to my failing eyes, practically brushing my nose; and then go on and do what needed to be done.

I built the fire so we'd live long enough to make such scenarios more than academic. And, choked by the boy's unread words, I burned all of them. Even though Flora wailed and had to be shoved back. Even though it'd be wiser to save some for later.

I burned them to silence him. At that age somebody ought to have done me the same courtesy. Fantasising all the while that it was my own past going up in flames, rather than my daughter's future.

The modest fire inspired the ice below us, so it seemed to glow from within its frosted depths. Rolling back the killing cold from the air made our bodies sluggish, dozy. If it hadn't been for our fight I'd have plunged irresistibly into a nap. Mostly to avoid Flora's accusatory glare, I got back down on my knees to examine the floor.

A blue filmy eye stared back.

'Jesus!'

I fell over backward. Curiosity trumped animosity; Flora slouched over to look, too.

'What is that? Are they *people* down there?'

A touch embarrassed, my old heart slamming about, I righted myself. It had been a shock. That was all.

'Not people, honey. Animals. Must be old, from when the waters froze and these ships got trapped.'

Way back, in the last flagging days of commerce, spotty electricity, and the rule of *homo sapiens*. The shapes were frozen in at least two meters down, maybe more. The ship had tilted; its hull squeezed, then cracked by tremendous force.

Bleating panic as water rushed in. A jumbled chaos of wool and frantically scrabbling feet. Nowhere to go in this horrendous piss-stinking metal box they'd been crammed into. Still the body struggled, because it wanted to live. Prolonged suffering.

When like a sonic boom the freeze whipped through heading for shore, some beasts were crushed just like the hull as the water abruptly solidified. The lucky few. An end too quick for comprehension. In the midst of pandemonium, a loud sort of clap inside your head, and then blessed oblivion. Nothing but a haze of expanding red.

Here finally were the grazing animals of history, just like in my books. I put my hand on the ice, imagining I could touch one on its woolly head to comfort them. They looked exactly as I'd dreamed of bringing triumphantly home on a spear. First to the Family; then anguished in the middle of the night to my own little family, for whom the stakes were so much higher.

I'd really been an idiot. Look at them locked away down there, forever unreachable. A whole ship of them and no good to anybody. Easy to sympathise with the mysterious artist, who'd knelt to chip away at the floor in dull obsession day after day. Only survival, the complete exhaustion of everything, had finally driven them off.

I wondered if the tongue-things huddled outside in the storm knew they had ancestors locked away in here. Likely they'd only see a resource to be exploited. Turn Flora and I into wet smears, then figure a way to drill down. That's what modern animals did. Found means to accomplishing everything humans couldn't.

Come morning, the storm didn't give up. Swaddling ourselves, Flora and I snuck outside to find the ship surrounded by dim lumps buried under snow. The migrating wave had halted all around us to wait it out. Downwind of the ship's shelter there were so many the ground looked bubbled.

What were they? I thought of huskies, had loved Jack London, but supposed all dogs were gone now.

The slashing wind and pebbly sleet didn't guarantee safety up here on the deck. As we peered fearfully over the rail at our predicament, the nearest hummocks stirred. What might have been a questing nose raised into the air. Difficult to discern, I had to keep wiping my goggles.

No missing what happened next. Whiskers bristled up like antennae. So many great whippy things amplifying each twitch of the increasingly active, interested head. Enough to scan the thoughts right out of your skull.

Petrified, we retreated. Peering from the doorway I saw it settle into an unremarkable lump once more, soothed by the storm's lullaby.

'That's right, you weird bastard,' I muttered. 'Nothing to see here. Back to sleep.'

Our fuel, the letters, all gone now. We ate the rest of the worms for breakfast, their insides gone gooshey from being frozen and thawed, pink slurry in a pale skin. I tried to warm mine over the lamp but it kept dripping in the oil, diluting it.

I paced the day out, round and round the inside of the ship. Circling the inside of my head in the same way. Tunning through possibilities for a way out. Every idea terminated in a solid frozen wall.

My daughter watched me thoughtfully. Calculatingly, one might say; if they didn't know and love her better. It was Flora who finally said what needed to be said.

'Daddy.'

Flora grabbed my arm as I was about to pass her for the hundredth time.

'Daddy, stop. We have to get out.'

'Those tongues-and-whiskers'll have us in chunks on the ice before we take two steps.'

'Then we'll … we'll move at night, when they're deeper asleep. The storm will cover us.'

'The storm will cover us, all right! Tuck us right up, it will!'

'Daddy you're not being helpful.'

'The very idea's barmy, nobody goes out at night. I still can't forget how poor Uncle Alessio got lost, caught out after sunset. He all but perished. Would have done, if Uncle Ebo hadn't nursed him three days running without a wink of sleep. He never came all the way back, either. The night took up residence behind his face.'

'Well we're going to become icicles anyhow.'

'If … if we're really going to try, we'll have to lose the sled. Even disembarking by the windward side the animals are packed together too densely. It'll be a miracle if you and I manage to squeeze our raggedy asses through, let alone dragging a toddler bath behind.'

'Ok.'

'Are we serious about this?'

'Serious.'

I bit my lip as we unpacked the sled. Old friend, it had travelled with us so far. The sight of it had always promised comforts: a bite of food, a mug of hot water, maybe a wash.

Now, emptied, it was merely a bit of nondescript pink/white plastic that had lived a hard life.

Flora worked impassively. If she felt anything, she wasn't keen to share. All we could take, we tucked under our clothes, and of the two of us I had the worst outfit for this. No proper outer shell to block the wind. I wanted my coat back, though I'd never ask for it. I wanted a better plan.

Once I became resigned to the outrageousness, nerves kicked in and I started babbling.

'Discard everything we can, to get the weight down. That. Yes, that too. If we sweat, we're dead.'

Pointless advice as Flora would be carrying far more than I. What she thrust on me were key things. The flint and steel. The tarps. I was touched by her uncharacteristic concern as she fussed over me, tucking them away. She must be nervous, too.

Where I put my foot down was insisting on being tied together.

'Really, Daddy?'

'It'll be a miracle if we're able to see much out there. And with the wind trying to rip our ears off we won't be able to hear, either.'

I held back the graphic detail that if an animal woke, the first I'd know about it would be a barbed tongue punching through the back of my head and out my surprised face. We twisted the duck sheet to make a rope between us. It had seen better days, I could only hope it would hold.

We weren't going to get any more prepared. At the top of the stairs I eased the battered door open for a peek, careful not to let it bang. Did I say we wouldn't be able to see much at night? It was a solid wall of black out there.

My whole body recoiled from the cold, trying to shrivel up. A gleeful flurry of ice crystals hit me directly in the face—not a good omen. I made ready to snuff the lamp.

'Are you ready, baby?'

'Wait.'

Flora had her knife out, which was really a screwdriver but I'd never told her that. I thought she was being a bit optimistic: knives were unlikely to accomplish much against the barbed horrors out there. Unless we decided to stab ourselves and get it over with.

'Daddy, hold the lamp over here.'

Right by the etched drawing, pretty much the last place in the universe I wanted to stand. With the tip of her "knife" Flora scratched FLORA in big serviceable block letters above the intricate drawing. Helvatica neue, I think. The font of chip packets and posters.

'The S.S. Flora,' I murmured. The ship shuddered in the storm, and the figure in the distance watched us intently over its shoulder. *Go ahead and leave*, it seemed to be saying with a sly wink. *See how much good it did me.*

With a violent move I snuffed the lamp.

'Let's go.'

Had I imagined myself in front, leading my daughter to safety? It was as dark as a clenched colon. My diminished eyesight was less than useless. The wind pushed us back and forth as Flora guided me to the rail. I could kind of see the rail, my hands on it. In the howling void below waited the animals.

Brave Flora hopped down first, then assisted me. A real leap of faith. It would probably have been easier if we weren't tied together, but damned if I was going to admit that now. I clutched the link like my last hope.

On the ice. My skin knew animals were all around us, even if the rest of my senses had clocked out. With an impatient tug on the rope, Flora got us moving.

Each whisker-tongue had to be navigated past on the windward side. Those long antennae would be sweeping lazily downwind, game over to get tangled in those. I missed the sled's loyal weight right away. The wind keened to scrape people, ships, and not-dogs clean off the face of the earth.

My advice had been pointless. Sweat poured off me, soaked my inner clothes, pure terror stink. Attuned to her environment Flora moved confidently, and I followed. Step forward. Shuffle right. Half step.

Why had she stopped? With an angry jabbing gesture she directed my attention to the snow mound directly in front of us. I had to bow close to see.

This one had its massive head and paws? hooves? tucked cosily inside the shredded remains of Flora's jacket, for all the world like a pillow. I only imagined the purring.

I shook my head emphatically.

—leave it!—

She pointed again and shook her fist, I could feel impulsiveness boiling off her. I physically blocked her with my body.

—no—

Not sure what she'd do. Until finally she started moving again, and I almost peed my pants in relief. The rope tugged taut and I was on my way. Shuffle step.

Then we were clear. No more snow-shapes around us, sensed more than seen until you took one step more and they were right on top of you. Only those receding behind. The storm covered them up.

Flora stopped and turned back to me, raising her hand. I stepped closer, thinking she was trying to celebrate. A glint. The screwdriver.

—she was going to stab me—
I flinched.
Stab me.
My little girl.

Abject before that raised hand, forced to confront what had been growing in me like cancer for some time. I was afraid of Flora. Afraid of my daughter.

I think she knew. I blessed the storm; I didn't have to see if she smiled.

With a violent stab Flora parted the rotten duck-rope between us and vanished.

FLORA & JIM

Chapter Six

The Moss Trap

I RAN THE cut rope dumbly through my fingers. Expecting my little girl to just *be* where she was supposed to be, safe on the other end.

You lost her, you lost her, shrieked the wind, screaming and pummelling me with sleet. Inconsolable. Years of Mai's petty torment for naught now I'd gone and done the worst thing, the very worst.

During our marriage she had never stooped to violence,

although I'm sure she was tempted. Magnitudes fiercer than some kid raised with his nose in a book. Well, I wasn't that kid now. No longer even a father. Flora had gone, off chasing her "Fauna".

And because I was horrible, awful, I staggered against the wind and contemplated being free. So light with it I could whirl up and away into the churning clouds. Undone from the anxiety that had squeezed my chest every second since Flora's arrival in this world.

No—earlier. Since Mai had turned baleful eyes my way to hiss, 'I'm pregnant!' Her whole body tensed with the longing to strike me. That brought on the panic: Mai was the smart one and briefly she didn't know what to do.

A wrinkled baby's face, like a pickled nut. My daughter. I'd thought I wanted a boy, until the moment I saw Flora and knew it could never have been anyone else. How casually her tissue-paper existence might tear, by slip or inattention.

Now suddenly as if by dark magic all I had to look out for, please, make happy, was myself! Rebounded right back into the shape of my old life, as though it had been waiting for me.

I could even ease myself down onto the ice right here. Let the cold come in and everything stop. It would be like slipping into the library, taking down a book and closing the door. An end I'd secretly desired ever since that first night lying in unfamiliar darkness, my gut straining with purloined food, Mai snoring beside.

Nobody had come after us. Not even Aunt Abena. She always came, that's what she *did*. That's when I finally and truly understood how irrevocably I'd given up books, safety and Family.

Caught in the dream of the cut rope I only paused a second, but the storm was no place for standing still. Already I was reeling. Tipsy as my blood began to settle. Bye bye, brain. Chips of ice rattled against my face like rice, like ice. Oh Mai, I so wanted to throw rice at our wedding. Crazy joyous idea, wasting food.

Terrifying to even suggest it to her. Give me animals and a spear any day.

I gingerly approached the topic after three days of hiking. Three fruitless days since we left the Family. Searching listlessly for districts that rang some kind of bell; following the memory of a girl who'd been very small, traumatised, and angry.

I'd watched Mai daydream of running from the dastardly Family straight into her parents' loving arms. This protracted search was beginning to weigh her spirit. Only yesterday, chewing her lip, she'd asked if I thought she'd done something wrong.

Baffled as to the answer she might be fishing for, I tried, 'It doesn't sound likely. What do you mean, "wrong"?'

—*wrong tone, jim. too sucky*—

'Wrong as in bad. It's like I've done something wrong, and they're hiding from me.'

The sullen child she'd been still so close. So quick to turn wrathful in the face of my unhelpful puzzlement. We were both so young.

'It's nothing, forget it.'

Of course, we weren't *quite* up to suggesting she might not have memorised the route clearly. Under duress, etcetera. No, that would spark the righteously offended rage in my Mai. I wanted to bring her something nice, not make it worse.

It's nothing, forget it. Walk on. Already our feet hurt. Following survival manuals I pressed finger and toenails each evening to check they'd remained pink. I moved confidently. I worried. Intellectually, I knew things were going to get worse if we didn't find her parents soon, but had no frame of reference to how that would actually look.

Mirroring my false courage, mornings were when Mai's ebullience shone brightest. Skipping out with a cheery, 'Today's the day!' or, 'I can't wait to hug my Mum. I bet I'm taller than her now!' before I'd finished packing. Energy that dipped rapidly, faced with the reality of walking.

I timed my approach for the morning break. Already we were on the downhill slide: Mai sat on a slab of concrete with her back to me, moodily kicking at the dust.

Tender for her disappointment I rubbed the back of her woollen balaclava. Mai stiffened, then sighed and slumped into the caress with what I liked to assume was more affection than resignation.

'Honey?' I ventured.

'Gah!'

Mai shot to her feet, stalked off a few steps.

'Why do you always spoil it with words? I'd be better off doing this on my own!'

Empty threats, I knew, they bounced off. Mai didn't have it in her to creep off and leave me behind. The company of her thoughts was its own purgatory.

—*empty threats, they struck*—

I held out my hands placating.

'It'll be alright, baby. We'll find them.'

Toothless promise. I wanted to add, 'Your Dad will be there, tall with a thin moustache just like you said. Better at medicine than that cranky fraud Uncle Isaiah ever was. Ready to deliver a baby. Your Mum with hair like water; kinder than Uncle Ebo, fiercer than Aunt Abena. A mother not too stern to say she was proud.

'They'll point and shout and start running toward us, laughing incredulously. They'll be so happy. You'll be happy. Holding you and his wife, your Dad will give me a stiff respectful nod, man to man, tears of joy in his eyes. And bringing their little girl home will be the proudest moment of my life.'

But Mai's right. I ruin it with words. Her eyes softened forgivingly, and I mustered courage, such as it was.

'Mai, will you marry me?'

She ripped off her balaclava to stare. That's what we did with other people, we showed our faces. To reassure. Or confront.

'Honey, don't, your face'll get cold.'

'You think we should *what*?'

'Get ... married?'

'To each other.'

'Well we're going to have a baby.'

I'd birthed the concept for myself by saying it out loud. Now it firmed.

'I think we should get married.'

Mai wrung her headgear like she wanted to strangle it. Walked in a little circle. I stood by and waited patiently, even if my insides were a twisting stew.

—you knew how to make your face stone while you were thinking. giving nothing away—

—so good, you cursed your daughter with it permanently—

'Ok,' she answered finally, turning back, and my heart kicked.

'You mean ...'

'Ok, Jim, I'll marry you. But let's wait 'til we find my parents. I want Daddy to give me away.'

I hadn't really thought she'd say yes. Not strong willed Mai. I almost knocked us both flying in my rush to wind her in my arms. Mai laughed, that delighted unselfconscious honk I loved so much. And I was kissing my bride, kissing the warmth back into her cold face.

I hadn't been able to throw rice at our wedding; and then painstakingly pick it up afterward. Or see my Mai radiant in a gorgeous dress. Or any of the other things I wanted to give her.

The patter of ice felt less vicious. That or my extremities were peeling off. But the wind now seemed to push from behind instead of against me, urging me to go after our daughter. A shitty father, yes. There was no one else, so the wind wouldn't let me rest. It whined.

—if it were your child you'd never give up and you'd never stop looking—
—a hole where my family should be—
—i, jim, take you, mai—
And the last, like a shard of ice in my heart.
—jim! something's got me!—

Though my eyes were shuttering I began trudging in what I hoped was the right direction. Flora certainly thought so when she ran off this way. Even though she was making a huge mistake.

Even now, when the wind might whittle me down to my teeth, I could hardly blame her. Like any new-minted teenager my daughter was impassioned. Wanted life to be better. It's only when that dries and flakes away that folk become adults; the process is of loss as much as gain.

No blame. I couldn't forgive, either. To truly let go I'd have to extend the same to my younger self who'd acted no less nobly, chasing after ideals and other ghosts. Ending up being pursued in turn. He could go to hell. He'd condemned me there, right enough.

I shook my fuddled head angrily, a groggy back and forth. Past or future, I didn't matter. The storm's determination to knock me down didn't matter. Not while Flora was sprinting to some kind of Alfred showdown. What mattered was catching up with my baby girl before something terrible happened.

Progress was slow. Breathing stopped up, and with maddening frequency I had to struggle to eject plugs of boogerice, the next crusting as soon as the last popped free. Agonising for hairs and soft tissue, getting stripped over and over. *Just die*, I willed the nerves of my face.

I rolled one plug between mittened fingers, holding it right close to see. They were coming out red now, Mai's favourite colour. And, you know, they *were* organic material. The breakfast worms had been a lifetime ago. Quickly before I could overthink, I fumbled the maroon pellet into my gob and swallowed. The idea of eating would have to be enough.

Soon avoiding suffocation became quite the triumph. The blast at my back didn't just drive frost through my clothing like nails, oh no, that would be a friggin' holiday. Ice built up until I was labouring under the growing useless weight.

Sealed in an exhausting carapace. Blind, not that there was anything to lay peepers on. And sickly afraid that should I prise free, my face might lift along with balaclava and goggles. Eyelids stretching like taffy.

To raise either arm to the height of my face was wildly too much to think of, anyhow. Lurching ahead, on jointless limbs I took on faith were still down there, clomping feet scarce cleared the ground. Should I trip I'd float down, down through a morass of lassitude. Float for cold dreamy years, then shatter.

I couldn't help but be aware of my breathing: cold jets drawn into my head to stab my brain. Forced out with a little more of my life going with them. You can't get enough air through nostrils at the best of times. The exertion I was under made it torturous.

—keep going—

An automaton of suffering. All that idealism and hot pumping life I'd been formed of had slowed since I left the Family. Sluggish ice in my veins. The dimming sparks of injustice at my core seemed so far away. Now, finally, I was one of the Family.

This was the timeless lonely wasteland they'd seen for humanity's future. A cold hell nobody in their right mind would condemn a child to. No more babies. Not ever. It's not so bad, Jim. You just lie yourself down, and decide that's as far as you go.

This made me long ever harder for the child I'd been and I sobbed behind sealed lips, wanting the impossible. For Uncle Ebo to sweep me up and explain these horrors away. And for Aunt Abena to stand between me and the cruel wind, where she'd always stood. I'd once measured myself against Uncle Ebo's bulk. *You wanted more weight? You wanted to know what it was like to be an adult?*

Not above pressing my ear to closed doors, me.

'I want the boy to be better, to fulfil his potential,' Aunt Abena had argued after I'd been on the receiving end of yet another public shaming. I listened, and I shook with mute humiliation and rage, slow boiling rage. This was what sneaking away from chores got me. All my fault, like Mai had nothing to do with it.

Abena had not been gentle to her own sons, either, and now they were gone. I tried not to feel smug about that because that was the nastiest. A muffled sound of frustration. Uncle Ebo quietly responded, 'I just want him to be happy.'

Both long-dead because of me. Which with the delirium of fatigue I blamed them for. Shouldn't they have stopped all this? Couldn't they see that skinny bookworm, how weak and useless I was? "Fulfil my potential," that was a laugh. Should never have loved me enough to let me leave. Loved me more than the whole Family.

Wretched resentment clomped my feet forward. I was stomping on their faces while they looked back at me with love, only love. Stopping was no longer an option. I should've lain down at the start when I had the chance. I shuffled on, waiting for something to take pity and put an end to my march.

As it must've taken Flora, the wind took me thus the rest of the way across the ice. Then it died. The dull cannonade against the outside of my ice shell stopped. I'm sure the crunch underfoot changed when I staggered from sea onto beach but, locked away from the world, I couldn't hear it.

One thing: milky light through eyelids. Dawn was breaking out there. I raised my leaden head and sniffed feebly through my only holes to outside: smoke. I could follow smoke.

Ask and ye shall receive. In the protected lee of two boulders I found the remains of a fire pit by crashing face-down into it. That stopped me, all right, with a nose full of ash.

The other father, his fat son, and my daughter had moved on. I'd missed the shindig. That might be my life now; alone, chasing, always following and unable to reach them. While they travelled on ahead to the best of everything, proud Alfred leading the way, and Flora and Fauna hand in hand.

The pit's warmth ought to have been agonising. That it wasn't made me rock side to side, moaning inside my ice caul. Even if I'd the means I couldn't rekindle Alfred's fire, my hands were useless.

I tucked them into the hot ash with my body balled over them. Grovelling in the smut and praying for the return of pain. Reality slunk away.

That little sketch of a fire saved my life. I was lucky to wake. Muddled, thought I was coming to in the stone lobby of that cheap apartment block back in the city. The wind was shrilling in the equipment outside. Mourning the loss of children who'd know how to come play.

We couldn't run and jump, but we'd been snug in the pond listening to it. No—we'd been sick. That was right, I remembered now. And if I didn't find the strength to crawl across and clean my daughter, get some meltwater into her, she'd die.

The play equipment wailed.

'Sss ok, Flora,' I slurred, pulling myself to my knees. All head to toe in crumbly ash. 'Sss just the wind.'

Sodden balaclava and goggles cast to one side, I pressed both cheeks with my palms. There was still some feeling in the heel of each, to clue me in to what my face was up to.

Astonishingly, with the caul melted away into the fire pit I could open my eyes. Could even see out of one of them, albeit murkily. Hesitant to press my luck with the blind one, picturing it erupting as it warmed and running down my heedless cheek.

That was ok. One eye was more than I'd been expecting. Without sight I'd have of course gone blundering down the beach regardless, but in an unfamiliar environment my chances wouldn't have looked good. One eye was the great wash of knee-weakening relief that I could make this work.

'Ok,' I breathed. 'Ok. I'm going to get up and keep going.'

I couldn't take the time to go pulling boots and gloves off to check digits. Odds were I'd never get them on again. Envisaged a future wiping my ass with a dead flipper.

Truthfully now was the worst time to move. Defrosted tissue was horribly vulnerable to refreezing until it healed; the damage would spread exponentially. Were I home, the Family's scouts would never allow it.

But the screaming hadn't been part of any dream, and no wind ever cried with such outrage. The whole of lost humanity protesting with this one voice. Somewhere nearby, somewhere echo-y and eerie. Even with the distortion, I knew that voice better than my own.

Balancing on stilts that used to be real legs with knees. Hands in my armpits to keep them safe. Gone so easily from a suffering machine to an engine running on hate. Make my daughter scream, would you? Scare my little girl? Alfred wasn't having Flora. After all this, I refused to be left with nothing.

Back around the rocks. In the thin dawn light, the desolation I'd come to became clear. Sea and land had finally ceased their conflict and lain down together.

Advancing in hissing gusts, the sand had spread out vastly with no plants to hold it. I didn't often ponder how the soil must have changed, because everywhere I'd lived had been largely concreted over.

In fits and starts I journeyed down the flat, cold-locked beach. All before me the same uniform heartless grey. If I gathered enough ash to fling into the air, watch it settle horizon to horizon, it could hardly look different. With my own coating I fit right in.

I stubbed my toe and glanced down, alerted more by interrupted progress than any sensation. Dull terracotta in the drifts. A brick! Well now we were getting somewhere. Pincering it between mittens I gathered it up and wiped it off, for the comfort of colour as much as a weapon.

The other father was going to be sorry. My new friend and I continued on, though if it hadn't been for the screams I'd have assumed we were going the wrong way. The beach looked like nobody had ever visited. A great place to wait out the end of the world.

Finally el-brick-o and I came upon a drain pipe poking out of the sand. Innocuous, like all the old world's infrastructure had been; couldn't have beachcombers asking awkward questions about, say, the environment.

Flora's voice had echoed. This was it. I pushed the brick in with both hands.

'What's it look like?'

Brick didn't have an opinion.

I had to crouch to peer in for myself. Streams of wastewater had once flowed through here heading out to sea. When I crept in the opening I found the floor was a slick toxic mess. Oily colour swam on every surface, wanting to distract, seduce. Oddly, it seemed to be the pollution that had preserved the pipe so well, by hardening into a protective coat.

I hesitated, one foot in. You can't go too far underground. The soil is so frosty down there it clangs like an iron gate when struck. Another screech decided the matter.

—*keep yelling, baby. you're alive*—

Luckily I didn't have to duck and scurry far. The tunnel quickly opened up into a broad underground concrete basin with a path or lip around. Lit by a shaft that punched up through the ceiling to the remains of a corroded grate.

My vision was shot, and as I tottered upright I struggled to make sense of what I was seeing. Colour? Not the tunnel's oily slick, this was verdant and natural. Like an old photograph. Enough to put my humble brick to shame.

I wiped my face and things steadied. The steep basin seemed to be lined with a bright rich carpet. This explained why the other father hadn't been able to pass up venturing into such an uninviting hole.

Lichen and moss, the last living cousins of the land plants. The most precious thing you could imagine. A pinch a day, and Flora would spring up before my eyes. She deserved to be tall. The way Mai talked, all her family had been giants.

'*Dad-dee!*'

Flora croaked from the bottom of the basin, having hollered herself hoarse. I used to joke she'd do that, use her voice up, when she was a squawking baby. Look at my baby now. Standing shivering on one leg in my oversized coat, with the other ankle swelled askew from her fall into the basin, not right, not right at all.

And where was this fucker who ought to have been taking care of her? Right around the other side of the path Alfred hesitated in the act of dragging his son away, seeing me. They were flustered. What were they fleeing? Me?

We'd never been so close. The other father, straight-backed and proud with a backpack stuffed with plenty. Me, an ash-daubed shambling wreck. Staring with hungry eyes. Eye. Pockets excluded, I carried only my brick. I struggled to understand why they were running.

'*Don't leave me down here!*' Flora cried to them, but mainly to the boy. Of course she did. Alfred's son was more handsome than I could have imagined with his clean skin, young muscle filling out his frame. I felt embarrassed for my scraggly girl, my string bean girl crying out to him. I felt humiliated I hadn't done better.

Fauna frowned at her with regret, before turning and hastily retreating with his father. Flora screamed with such wretchedness it nearly broke me. They disappeared into a tunnel on the far side that could only lead deeper underground. Had I thought I hated him before? Now I hated with every part of me still able to feel.

—*yes, but what were they running from? wake up, jim!*—

Flora was answered. A guttural low clicking filled the concrete cavern.

—*jim-booo. turn around. you've got seconds to live*—

A looming shape detached from the wall, gaining definition as it came on. Hey, good news! Every fear that something's there, in the dark, is true! And it was an animal. Finally I came face to face with one.

What animal was it? A moving wall of dense waving fluff, or feathers. So colourless they'd taken on the appearance of the dimness and shadow behind. And something vividly orange at the top, hooked and cruel.

All I really caught in the oncoming torrent of fluff was the threat of that beaked opening mouth, hungry and ridged inside. The ridges were ... *vibrating*? Clicking? My brain zeroed in on what would hurt me to the exclusion of all else.

Now the beautiful grotto made sense. The moss was no blessing. It was a trap. Nourished by Fluffy's piss and the melting water generated. *Farmed*. Fluffy tended the trap, then sat back to see what came stumbling in.

Lucky us! Fluffy circled away from me, that avid beak pointed down toward Flora who shrieked defiance, shaking her fist at it. Briefly I thought my coating of ash had bought me time by confusing it. Then I realised I'd been discounted. Fluffy thought me too sick, too weak to bother with first.

It would kick off with the primary threat, the one raising hell. Then weak sick old me, sure, so I didn't feel left out. And perhaps slither off down the tunnel after Alfred and Fauna for dessert. I decided to cause a stink of my own.

'Hey, asshole!'

I banged the brick against the wall. Sorry buddy. Flora got wind of what I was trying and waved her arms.

'No! Down here! Leave Daddy alone!'

'Nah, you want a tasty bit of meat, don't'cha? Come and get it!'

That head whipped back around toward me like I'd stepped on its tail. This wasn't like my dreams of a hunterly conquest. Fluffy was *fast*. Wide staring eyes and a rictus mouth rushing at me out of the dimness.

In panic, I flung up both hands. A shock down my arm. My brain stuttering through attempts to keep up.

I don't suppose creatures like Fluffy had to worry about failure, second-guessing themselves into paralysis. It just snapped open that beak and did precisely as nature dictated. It survived.

Right up until my trusty brick cracked it between those beady eyes and the mountain collapsed at my feet. Fluffy thrashed and squealed, most of what had governed its life caved in. All hair fluffed out on end, doubling its size.

A seizure. I had to put it out of its misery. Through the squalling, all I could think was that Alfred should have been bold enough to stay and slay Fluffy himself. Then he could have done me, two birds with one stone.

The brick had done its duty. I stuck my knife through Fluffy's rapidly blinking eye, surely that would suffice. One eye for each of us now. The tremors increased, the clicking and screeching.

—*oh god, just die!*—

Until I wiggled the blade as hard as I could and caught something vital. Fluffy clenched rigid, beak straining wide. Then slowly collapsed to rest. Not exactly how I'd dreamed: murdering an animal was traumatic. Every part of me wanted to be shed and burned.

'Daddy?' Flora called tremulously. 'Daddy, is it dead?'

It was. I'd done it.

'I'm coming, sweetheart.'

I couldn't reach Flora without slithering in myself. Another rope to be made—my shirt? Might be too rotten to hold, casting her back on that bung ankle. I was too tired to think.

'Wait, my hair.'

Matted, stiff with filth, she held it up above her head.

I nudged my smeared brick aside, seized the plait and yanked with all I had. Feeling muscles part and fail in my back. We almost ended up at the bottom together. She came reluctantly, my Flora, clawing puffs of moss from the wall as though she did not want to be saved.

We both sat panting on the hard floor. The corpse of Fluffy between us. I wanted to stroke that mane, so soft. Refrained superstitiously in case the shuddering and squealing started again; dead, definitely dead.

Considering we made landfall fatally separated and with nothing but what we carried, I thought we'd done surprisingly well. Well, I could see why Flora wouldn't rush to agree. She sat like a stone, her eyes bruised wells into nowhere. I had to try something.

'I'm so sorry about Alfred and your Fauna. Honey, I've not been trying to catch them cause we're bad people.'

'*They're* the bad ones!' she barked with an angry jerk of her head at the tunnel they'd vanished down. 'They left me to die! Fauna left me …'

False idols toppled, I ought to be dancing a jig. The death of her childlike affection was more than I could stand. How Flora's untried heart must have fluttered, standing next to her white knight at last.

'It's more complicated than that, baby. Folk have to look after their own. They have to make choices that aren't fun about where they belong, what's most important. And sometimes because of that they end up doing … dreadful things. Even when they don't mean it to turn out that way. Doesn't make them *bad*. Not really.'

Her eyes bore into mine angrily.

'They *are*!'

'Oh honey. They're just people like the rest of us. You wouldn't go saying your Mum was bad, would you?'

'No.'

Sullenly. Get to the point, old man.

'Of course not. She was the best and we miss her very much. Well, she didn't mean to, but she ended up doing the worst thing I've ever heard of.'

'This is it!' Mai cried, elated.

All I saw was another intersection. Same as the hundred other dispiriting heaps of rubble we'd hiked through. Only our tracks in the dust to prove we hadn't been past already.

The wind mysteriously absent these nights, I glanced back often at the trail we left. I guess some part of me kept hoping the Family would be coming after us. Hope springs eternal, to eternal chagrin.

This search had dragged too long and our stolen food was mostly gone. I understood starvation on an intellectual level, Uncle Ebo had never let it closer than that. I knew enough to dread it. Babies needed food to grow. I couldn't deliver Mai to her parents short their grandchild, they'd never want me then.

So the relief when Mai finally recognised something was incredible, even at this late hour.

'Great!' I said, puffing up to join her. 'We can be with them first thing tomorrow morning.'

'What? We're going now!'

I eyed the length of the shadows.

'Mai, I don't think ...'

She was off before I'd finished. A trot that evolved into a run. Mai was fearless and bold, rushed ahead. Away from me toward warmth and love and family. She also didn't have to try running with a wheelbarrow.

'Mai! We don't have time!'

The breeze stirred as the temperature fell and still I chased her.

'Mum?' Mai called. 'Dad?'

Buildings watched us, still and silent, and nobody answered. It was rapidly becoming too dark to see. Good. If we were to perish here, so close to our goal, I didn't want to see.

'In here!'

Suddenly popping up, Mai grabbed my arm, the wheelbarrow tipping over. Leave it, no time now. We banged through a door. Thank God she hadn't left me behind. A short stop from losing sight of her to fearing she'd made good on that threat.

We were in what had perhaps been some kind of commercial kitchen. Hard to see without light. Mai was already pushing her way through to the back room, calling, 'Dad? Mum?' Banging into things and swearing. I followed.

It was cold. That was my first clue something was wrong. It shouldn't be cold. Cold was for outside. '*Unnaturally quiet*,' Ebo had said. '*Straight away that wasn't right.*' Every hair stood straight out through my clothes like quills.

I fumbled the lamp out and lit it, having to make three tries, my hands were shaking so much. Mai snatched it from me and stepped into the other room. I considered the dark and painful cold outside as a valid option. Love alone drew me after her.

Frost had come in, climbing up the walls. The little crystals glittered. Every surface of the room gleamed, and if the cold hadn't been biting at my face I would have found it enchanting.

Not excluded were the two figures kneeling in the centre, their foreheads touching. They were tall. The man had a thin moustache. I'd no doubt that beneath its fairy dusting of frost, the woman's long hair was shining.

Holding the lamp high to see, to make herself see, Mai began to shudder. A grinding sound deep in her chest, of broken things rubbing together. It cracked the hushed perfection of the room.

The two statues curved over a blank space between them. Protecting it. This was where the Family had taken Mai from as a wailing child. From her parents, who were already very dead. Frozen forever in the act of protecting her with their last embrace.

With wooden movements my Mai tried to insert herself back into that void, into their arms, but she'd grown too big. There was a hole in her heart where her family should be. A hole in their arms she could never return to.

That night the wind returned with a vengeance and we had to stay right there with her parents' sightless eyes looking on. Outside in the street our footprints were swept clean. We would never be found.

Once she had cried herself into an empty, staring husk I put Mai to bed and held her in the blankets. I whispered in her ear.

'I, Jim, take you, Mai, to be my lawful wedded wife.'

Her father was here. That would have to be close enough to giving her away. With them glittering at the centre of the room as witnesses I promised Mai she'd be safe, taken care of. I promised she wouldn't be alone. And meant every word, with the strength of heart that came from zero consideration of how I'd manage it.

We didn't have any rings. Constricting blood flow around your fingers would just help them fall off. I circled her finger with mine instead, and Mai buried her face in my shoulder. Trusting me this once.

'Mai kept your grandparents alive in her memory through sheer force of her considerable will. Made them live for me, too, so vividly I was halfway to loving them, these people I'd never met.'

That was the tale I told Flora. How thinking there'd be a new life for her at the end of the rainbow, a better life with Mai's parents, led me to betray the Family.

And how Mai betrayed me in turn by never being able to admit, even to herself, that her family was dead. That my Family saved her. Not once through all those years we grew up together, the big and small kindnesses. Not until the truth was staring her in the face.

I told Flora I'd forgiven her mother. That what Mai did wasn't too terrible to let go, not when you love someone. Mai wasn't a bad person.

—only my heart knew it was a lie—

FLORA & JIM

Chapter Seven

Gourmet

Sitting panting in that drain, a wet brick by my feet, I knew I had to get on with butchering Fluffy while it was still warm. In fatigued memory I scrabbled to recall what tales of wilderness claimed could be handily crafted from animal parts. For sure there was a knack to it.

The very idea of that first cut made stinging bile back up my throat. Though I tried to disguise it, I kept turning away to retch. Agony twisting my empty guts. The guts. We had to get

Fluffy's guts out first. Without puncturing them.

—*just start cutting, jim. nobody's going to do it for you*—

Between the hind and up, blubbery lips peeling away from my slice. The belly was spotty: thumbprint-sized strawberry freckles. I thought of Dalmatians, and the cruel socialite who'd wanted their skin—for luxury, not survival.

A weird balloon-piercing "pop" as I penetrated the abdomen and Flora, who'd crept up fascinated, recoiled sharply with a hand over her lips.

'What is it honey?'

'That stench!'

That was when I started to worry about what had happened to my face. Not that gnawing at troubles did any good; they sure wouldn't magically restore a ruined nose.

To our left I made a slippery pyramid of whatever came loose from inside Fluffy when I yanked. Steaming hot in my hands; warmth wasted on the ravaged fingers, but a morbid treat to the wrists.

—*get on with it!*—

Tried to make sense of the liver. These globs lacked the illustrated anatomy labels my study had made me used to— could it be the jaundiced purse? The bruised purple slab? Put them both aside. According to lore, munching on carnivore liver had spelled the grim shitting end of more than one historic adventure.

Doubtless in this new world of bioaccumulation, the risk of sticking the wrong thing in your mouth was so much higher. My nether exit felt weak just remembering what had happened to us in the red-threaded industrial district.

The dun mush I experimentally squeezed from Fluffy's scarred intestine came speckled with a bright constellation of tiny plastic. Looked like the beasts could adapt and adapt and adapt; but in the end there was no outracing civilisation.

Last laugh to us.

Like animals ourselves Flora and I snacked straight from the steaming carcass as we worked. Cutting gooey wads of tissue to tuck in our gaunt cheeks. We couldn't help it. A row of sagging spotty nipples peeked through the soft belly fur, which likely made Fluffy female; Flora severed one with a grunt of delight. A veiny treat she could scarce cram in her mouth.

Prissy young-me would've been in fits of revulsion. Truthfully once you got hungry enough, there wasn't much to it. Chewy dampness. A sort of glowy spreading systemic relief as you choked the bolus down. *Feed me more*, my stomach begged.

It wouldn't be until later I found the destruction of my nose had carried off taste along with smell. Ought to have felt a blessing, given the circumstance. But what fool ever celebrated having something taken away.

Blood sent out tendrils across the floor, with crystal flakes forming at the edges. I was reminded of the frost covering Flora's maternal grandparents, kneeling in their dark and silent room. Obediently trailing gravity, the blood ran down into the garden Fluffy had so diligently tended, as a last gift.

A waste, from our point of view, but what could we do? We'd nothing big enough to collect it in for cooking. A bellyful of raw blood would do neither of us any good. Already wistfully wondering if we might have somehow brought the sled. Never mind we were damned lucky to make it here at all.

Our next step, peeling hide from flesh, was the most upsetting. Flora grabbed hold of Fluffy's hind legs and at first the skin pulled off, easy peasy. A yellow membrane parting from plum-dark flesh and striations of bone.

Then, as the body grew colder it began to resist, protesting the theft of its covering. I found myself having to cut more and more. The hide off the forequarters ended up quite raggedy.

Four limbs. Roughly familiar joints.

Flora was frowning at Fluffy as though trying to recall something sickening, that hovered just outside memory. Every bit as bad as a stomach full of blood.

'It looks like a person, Daddy.'

'I know, honey. Just ... don't think about it. We'll get through.'

A few more slices and I held up the bloodied result, flapping it triumphantly. Briefly I draped the hide furry side down across Flora's narrow shoulders.

'You'll look like a proper princes when we're done. Snug as a bug.'

Wishful thinking perhaps, but for a moment the worry and sorrow in her young eyes lifted. Promise that in the future my girl might get past her disappointment. She stroked the fur tentatively.

'It's warm!'

'That's the idea.'

Pride was going to split me right open.

—*warmer than any fire, hey alfred, you fucker. who's the provider now?*—

Laying the hide flat, hair side down, I directed Flora to stand on one end to stretch it out which she did, favouring her ankle, with me at the other. I wasn't the only one sneaking greedy peeks at Fluffy's gleaming carcass waiting off to the side. Fluffy's eye watched us right back from that meat-snarl of a face. Critical of how we treated her glory.

Reaching in, we both got busy scraping as much goop off the wet side of the hide as possible. Less of a job for knives (especially when one is a Phillips head); even dull as our tools, too easy to pop through and ruin the job. So we scraped away with our fingernails.

The sensation wasn't my favourite. I quivered as though they scratch-scratched down my own back.

'Ok, enough brawn. The final stage needs brains.'
I'd already done the hard work of opening Fluffy's head.
—*thanks brick!*—
Now I lifted that massive beaked cranium onto my knees and slit the thin covering. Picked out bone shards to get at the grey goodies beneath. As much as I knew Fluffy was just an animal, it was still deeply sobering to let the jellied consequence of my violence drip through my fingers.

There was a story I'd constructed that allowed me to get up off the floor of a morning: son, scholar, lover, husband, father. Nice easy trajectory. I've never claimed perfection, I've blundered into mistakes. But in no direction have I ever envisaged myself a drooling maniac flailing about with his fists.

I'd acted in great need. In danger. Now I felt sick, as though I'd done this to another person. Crushed their hopes and dreams in a spray of red.

—*that's not me. i'm not the man who does that*—
'Daddy? Daddy, come on.'
'What?'
'You've been sitting there staring at it.'
Vaguing out. That was supposed to be Flora's job. I shook myself back into action, feeling too keenly how inactivity had invited stiffness and weariness over the threshold.

There. Sawing through spine to get the skull out was almost the end for my knife, but left enough brainpan to suffice as a sort of pot, if I plugged holes with rags and worked in small batches. Now we needed liquid water.

I was no Alfred, sadly, with whatever he had to burn in such miraculous quantities. Before we lost the light entirely I dispatched Flora to gather char from the seaside pit where I came ashore. She returned limping and muttering with it scooped into her shirt.

To nourish a fire we sacrificed lichen, harvesting carefully from the basin lip where the garden was dried and crumbling. Porous chunks of concrete came off in our hands and had to be sifted out. The luxurious growth had been eating into it, possibly across many generations.

With lichen as a starter we burned bone shards, sheafs of our hair, even the long dreadlock that'd saved Flora's life. Hopefully she wouldn't fall into any more pits. Shivering, we wrapped ourselves in tarps and even donated what clothing we could spare, promising we'd replace it with something better. All we couldn't eat or use.

Fluffy's beak sneered at me from the heart of the precious nest of coals.

—*you'll see*—

In our cups and brain pan dish I cringingly mulched handfuls of cold brain and lukewarm water into a scummy goo. Then, like a cream, we worked it into Fluffy's skin. That was the big secret to preserving hide: rubbing in brains. Thank goodness it wasn't more complicated or I'd never have remembered.

The mix made numb fingers slippery. The digits had been good sports, responding haltingly to commands; still, I had to watch to be sure what they were up to. Tended to curl into odd spidery shapes without instruction.

An odd bit of nostalgia intruded. Reaching across, I gently dabbed the tanning goo on Flora's dry, cracked nostrils. She threw her head back in alarm until she realised what I was doing.

'There, honey. That's better, isn't it.'

She nodded mutely. Her eyes still all sad. A great wave of shame swelled up my throat.

'Flora—do you remember that tube of nose cream we had? I knew that was the last of it, and I used it anyway. I'm so sorry.'

Was that true? I'd no idea—I was so tired. A likely scenario, though: me furtively pocketing the empty tube. A foolish wish those last dabs might be magically regenerated when I pulled it back out. The sort of sleight of hand Uncle Ebo had produced, an endless supply of comforts.

Clearly I was no Ebo. Instead, my pantomime of regret to my daughter who'd looked up at me with reproachful eyes. Was that me, truly? Real or fake, confession felt amazing. Like relaxing a muscle I hadn't known was tensed. The devil's temptation was to keep going.

Proximity to our modest fire kept Fluffy pliable enough that we could now turn our attention to butchery. It used to be an entire profession. Our efforts were not so elegant. By brute force we disassembled what had been a living, breathing creature into fist-sized chunks, that could be stacked closer to the entrance to freeze.

Each gleaming with a precious seam of fat, without which the protein would shoot uselessly through. Also generous lashings of tendon, arteries, all the rubbery bits we'd pick out of our sheepish smiles as best we could. Hardly the feast of delicacies my childhood cookbooks had promised; but the wiser adult eye saw days of contentment ahead.

By the time we finished, breathless and smeared, the light falling through the gap in the ceiling had mellowed. The drain took on a rich, goldy look. Hard to believe we'd been at this all day. Our own internal fires flared up from the gobbets cramping our bellies. Even sans the pond we'd survive.

Bolstered by a glow of profound satisfaction, I finally bit the bullet and dared take off my shoes. No excuses, Jim. News from that front wasn't great: the little piggies looked bloated, bloodless and white. I feared scratching up future courage to take them to market.

Uncle Isaiah had always done slice and dice duty for Family, deploying his smattering of snake oil. Always insisting on a stiff upper lip, from that very old, very defunct school of drowning feelings like puppies. And that was for the boys. The fairer sex ought to … do whatever, preferably someplace else. Probably bleeding or something.

It hadn't occurred in my youth, but how fascinating as an adult to ponder him reconciling world views with two Aunts dragging his dinner home.

Months after poor Uncle Alessio strayed out after sunfall it became painfully clear that, despite all care, those toes were never going to wake up and suck down their bloodflow. With unseemly glee Uncle Isaiah summoned him to the infirmary.

Really just Isaiah's room, where nobody trespassed of their own free will unless it was carried by last legs, preferably dying. Or dead, as Aunt Aaliyah said she'd be before setting one foot in "that crusty old ghoul's nest". I suppose the handwritten INFIRMARY sign made him feel important.

'Come on, Alessio, hop up on the table. Let's see those trotters. Frozen in July, amputate in Jan,' Isaiah coughed humourlessly. I knew he only spouted such rubbish, and ostentatiously sharpened that perfectly sharp long knife, for the perversity of scaring me into jelly. That it made Alessio whimper too only made me loathe the bony fossil more.

Isaiah. The only member of the Family who didn't benefit from my adult retrospective. Some people you can safely hate for eternity.

With a flourish Uncle Isaiah positioned the long knife across the top of Alessio's flinching left foot. I stared at the curling black hair on those toes: luxurious in length, yet hardly adequate to keep them warm and protected from what was about to happen. Evolution was so stupid.

'Hold it there, Jimmy.'

'What?'

'The knife. You volunteered to help, didn't you boy? So help!'

I glanced across at Uncle Ebo who stood holding Alessio's hand. No help there. This moment wasn't about me. Humiliating for a boy to comprehend. I pinched cold steel and closed my eyes.

Whump!

Isaiah brought a heavy tome down on the knife, almost mashing my paws in the process.

Tang!

Blade hit tabletop. Alessio jerked his leg away, all but hitting himself in the face with his knee. His three smallest toes popped off, lying forlornly in their whorls of hair.

The bones of the remaining two were broken, which according to Isaiah made cutting through a cakewalk. I've never heard any cake make the sounds Alessio did as Isaiah finished the job. He had to hold the knife his damned self, I wanted no further part in it.

'Oh don't be such a baby!' Isaiah snapped as he worked. Alessio quietened down obediently, but not because he wanted to. Which made *me* wish I was big enough to embed that heavy book in Isaiah's pinched vinegar face, tongue-tip poking out the corner as he concentrated. Too many people ordered Alessio about. He could work things out if you waited, he was just a bit slow.

Uncle Ebo waited by to gather Alessio into an embrace at the end and feed him a few precious sips of vodka.

'There you go, Alessio, clear as ice, that'll set you straight. What, more? Now you're *sure* you didn't orchestrate this whole debacle just for a taste? You wouldn't do that to old Ebo, would you?'

Uncle Alessio chortled gamely, his broad smooth face streaked in tears. Too quick to forgive the well-meaning for speaking to him like a child. Perhaps when suffering, we all don't mind becoming a bit childlike. I'd wasted my time charging toward adulthood.

The bandages on Alessio's feet wept. Wiping up, Isaiah picked up a toe and wiggled it about.

'What do you say we pickle this piggy in the bottle. For luck.'

Uncle Ebo sighed.

'Isaiah, it's good to know if I ever need a grotesque old fiend I know exactly where to come.'

'No?'

'No.'

'You don't want to stay, put the rest of that in some tea?'

'No Isaiah, I do not.'

Ebo helped Alessio hobble from the room. Nobody ever lingered longer than needed. The heavy amputation book was a dictionary, so I snagged it and crept back to the library to look up what "grotesque" meant. I couldn't have agreed more.

Now I was the grotesque one. Parts of my heel looked fractured and chipped like stone; I'd never heard of that happening before. Frozen in July—I feared January was coming. It might be better in the morning; most things were. I'd just have to wait and see.

And see I did. When I woke the skin was an angry blameful red. It blistered on hands and abused feet. Thick pitchy scabs would form over the coming weeks. Worse on toes than fingers, which indicated which way this was going. Never came back to feeling soft or warm. I missed the rich prickle of defrosting that reminded me I was alive.

We'd kept the hide flat overnight by simple expedient of sleeping on it. I checked our work and where it was trying to stiffen the last of the jellied brains got massaged in. We were supposed to smoke it next. A rubbing of ash would have to do.

Then we turned our attention to the moss bowl. Examining it, hands clasped behind my back, I was grateful for the morning's returning beam of light. While in shadows the drain's dimensions were hazy, and Flora a total mystery to me.

'What do you think, honey? Do we inherit it? Did well for Fluffy. She lived here, caught things.'

Quite a successful life, judging by the layer of fat that'd nestled under that piebald skin. Teats suggested there'd even been surplus to raise pups, or chicks, or however this weird new taxonomy worked. Fauna ought to have stayed. This could have been their loving new life together. Lost for want of courage.

—or did i chase it off?—

'We could live here. We could be safe.'

Flora passed through the beam of sunlight. Her balaclava was rolled up, a courtesy for discussion. Her face told me nothing.

I'm sure she understood what I was asking: to give up the pursuit. With the moss trap we didn't *need* the other father or his son any longer. Also I was concerned what pressing on might mean to her. Flora had travelled with them. For a brief time they had cared for her, and been family.

They had not done well, or been loyal, though. Not like me. I was a proper father.

'Strip it. All of it. We're taking it with us.'

'You don't have to decide now, honey. We could rest. Give your ankle some time ...'

'We're not letting them get away.'

She rolled her balaclava down. Discussion closed. Smug satisfaction on my behalf; dismay on hers. Or was it the other way around? The bad father. The faithless lover. My vengeful Flora. My soft suggestions meant about as much to her as they had to Mai.

Beneath its little beam of sunlight we left the rock bowl scraped as clean as old bones.

We elected to follow Alfred and Fauna aboveground rather than continuing below. Managed to do so tacitly without admitting how that ongoing tunnel filled us both with dread. They were bound to pop out eventually, and we didn't know the first thing about sewers or how to live there. They might set an ambush. There might be more Fluffies.

Ducking out of the drain pipe the same way we went in, but in circumstances vastly different. Me, struggling under a parcel of meat I'd soon have to ask my daughter to carry. Flora by my side, imperiously decked in fur. Even the desolate beach looked lovely today, in its own way.

'Do you see it, Daddy?'

As we stood surveying the clouds thinned briefly, light swelled, and my eye finally caught the artistry of Fluffy's work.

The moss trap had only been the smallest part. All the beach warped subtly to funnel passers-by in. The sand was scraped and built up. Every rock and feature pointed toward the pipe, placed carefully by that fearsome orange beak.

Doubtless my brick had, too, when I picked it up. The act must have steered me to the drain. Fluffy had sculpted a masterpiece of hunger using sight, feel, smell, and doubtless any other senses that hulking monster had possessed.

'I could have staggered blind up the beach and still ended up crawling into the pipe after you,' I marvelled.

Wouldn't that have been a sight; both eyes ruined to match my nose. Hard to ignore it, curled right in my field of vision.

Flora took a deep, refreshing breath of the icy air. She shuddered, once, as though throwing off something unpleasant.

'It doesn't matter anymore. Let's go.'

I carried my lucky brick, too, for a while. How could I let go? I'd finally done it. Finally caught an animal. Conked it on the head before it bit my ass to bits.

When I traced Mr Brick's rough contours I thought of Aunt Abena's rare smile, seen only once or twice in my lifetime. Achieve my potential, indeed! The best I could be! At least I was happy.

Of course I kept falling behind. Flora turned around, waited with decreasing patience for me to catch up. Until she burst out with, 'Give the stupid thing here. I'll carry it. Along with everything else.' Condemnation for wasting calories. She was a woman on a mission.

Because I'm a pointless optimist I kept a small bolus of lichen warm and safe in my pocket. Nourished it with dribbles. A tiny secret promise to myself and my daughter that when this chase was finally over, we could stop and make ourselves a home.

FLORA & JIM

Chapter Eight

Glacier

The glacier marked the end of the world. Crossed off months we lost traversing the tumbled landscape before it. One didn't approach the glacier; the glacier came to you. A slow oozing that only advanced in nightmares, once you got so worn down you had to sleep.

The way we trudged and trudged, and thought ourselves

growing nearer, well that was merely an illusion of the ice wall's vastness as it claimed the sky.

The glacier also locked moisture away in its jealous heart. Generous only with its nocturnal exhalation, when cold knives roared in the dark. Funny, in hindsight, how I'd always dreaded sunfall. Like a child. Things were so much crueller here, close to the wind's source. Poke a toe out, lose it instantly.

At least, I would if I had any left.

On the ground where ants like us crept, I tended to keep my eye down. Came over disoriented and tired if I glanced about too often: too similar to everything we'd crossed the water to escape. The old world must have been dishearteningly homogenous no matter where you travelled.

If nothing else the buildings stood better preserved on this side. They had benefited mightily from desiccation, and by seeing humanity driven out much earlier. Crackling with blue static shock, we could dig in walls for a bounty of studs to burn. On the flip side, days were wasted roaming door to door trying to coax forth a handful of insects, a dribble of water. Flora's face drew sharper, if that were even possible. So must mine. It hurt to lay down without the padding.

Paradise and wasteland both. Where the glacier lorded over all. Tickling across it, we went. Us and them: them, the other father and his son. Straggling ahead, just out of reach, but close. Ever so close, now.

Flora cleared her throat.

'When we hit the ice wall, they'll have nowhere to run.'

Said conversationally, one adult to another. No "Daddy." I glanced across, her woolly face ringed with the hide we'd won from Fluffy.

Whereas I came out of the ice crossing minus an eye, some fingers, all toes, and the tip of my nose curled like old leather, my daughter seemed taller. Impossibly stern and resolute.

Badgering her to eat the lichen had been so right. Even though after several soakings the best she could offer was "less bitter" and thank heaven for her expressionless face. She finally accepted sucking it down as a sort of hot jellied tea, to terminate my nagging more than anything. Savouring the warmth as I relished the sight of her drinking it.

Flora was sometimes hard to look at now. As though she'd become as blinding as the ice. And if I didn't know better, disturbingly psychic. Glances snuck sideways or head on, she always knew when I was studying her.

'What will you ask the other father, Daddy?' she asked brightly. 'When we catch up?'

I turtled into my collar to get away. Sinister as that light playful tone, Flora was only teasing. She did that. Teased me. Crept up on my blind side like a stalking animal and then unexpectedly huffed or chuckled. My arteries were loose and rubbery from the shocks.

I was proud of that luxurious fur stole that snugged her up safe, though. More than I'd ever been of anything. No sign of decay yet ... although I might not be best qualified to tell. We'd never been roses, but sometimes now Flora had to pinch her nose and remind me it was time for a wipe down.

'Stinky old goat,' I'd laugh shakily. 'Baa.' Hoping for that shadow of a smile.

If Flora's expression eluded before, these days my occluded sight met an utter blank. A blank that sometimes lunged from my blind side, chuckling grimly. I had to wait for her voice to get any read on emotion.

We waited as long as I could stretch it out. We journeyed, we marvelled, then cowered beneath the glacier; but in the end Flora was my Uncle Isaiah. She recommended cutting the nose off, too, at which I flinched away clutching it protectively.

Flora grinned. I saw it in her eyes, the tiny crinkle.

'What's the matter, Daddy? Don't you trust me?'

Imagined my creaky but loyal old body whittled piece by useless piece until Flora was towing a stump behind. Just enough left of me to suffer. I couldn't undo the moment she raised her screwdriver against me in the screaming heart of the storm, and from there the skein fell apart. I had no-one to confide my dread to.

I wanted to ask Alfred if he too was soured to the marrow. Did his failing flesh feel its star sinking, his son's rising bright? This blank enigma smiling at me and waiting to slice pieces off was my own blood, and I loved her with all the rawness of my heart. She was not what I intended. I feared that difference. I loved her anyway.

I couldn't help involuntarily pulling away, the cringing animal instinct to protect myself. Until Flora halted me with an iron hand clamped on my ankle.

'Shh, Daddy.'

She lopped off my toes and blighted fingers with the same aplomb she'd used on Fluffy. I half-expected her to pop one in her rapacious mouth. Thankfully there wasn't much bleeding, like my body had recognised a bad deal and was trying to distance itself. Bon voyage.

With the glacier filling the sky, we made the sort of reckless dash to catch Alfred that I'd never dared. Not eating, nor warming ourselves properly. Eager Flora always out in front, which was a relief: I could watch her. No more sneaking up on me. I stumbled along and studied her strength, those sure strides. The both of us nothing but shrivelled dark skin over sinew, mummified already, yet see her thrive. Memory was where I lived as I trudged after my daughter. It was my meat and drink, when all other trace was gone.

Perhaps all it took to capture the other father was to give up everything; in which case I was never going to win. I was surprisingly ok with that. What I told myself in rhythm with heavy steps was I would never have chosen Alfred over Flora, not ever.

I fell, as Flora bounded on ahead. Happened frequently now. Toes were fairly important, as it turned out. At least it was so cold that impacting the ground never hurt; though it strained my heart in some vague deep place that my daughter no longer stopped. She never came back for me.

Sometimes by the time I wobbled in with dark nipping at my cracked heels, camp would already be set and Flora sleeping, blissfully unconcerned.

The scream came as I struggled up. Soundtrack of my life. A hot-blooded screech of excitement that stirred me into a stumbling run. Flora had them! Both of them, pinned at bay against the wall.

True to her prediction, when Alfred and Fauna reached the ice wall they had nowhere left to flee. Not unless they could fold themselves into one of its many slender fluted cracks and vanish, like the ghosts they'd so often seemed to be.

Up close that mass of translucent flinty blue, banded in grey, was so subtle it really did seem as though you could trip and plunge into it. Dissolve.

Left up to reality to assert the glacier's surface as hard, cold, unforgiving. It seemed to soak up the light. The sickly feeling I'd seen a blue glow like that before snagged like an itch at the centre of my head. The gusts of chill that came off it were searing. They stupefied me.

Flora lunged, teasing, like an eager hound unsure where to bite first. There were so many wonderful choices. She was not asking them anything.

Bile, sudden and stinging. The exertion of catching them had almost finished me.

Alfred dragged his headgear off in one rough movement, to plead. Showing his common humanity, the very first bargaining point. The epicanthic fold lent a hardness to the man's stare, but finally I was almost on top of him, and I could see it came from fear. Not fear for himself. For his son, thrust behind him for protection.

A weathered face. Hollowed by tiredness and desperation. A map of the futile chase we'd endured, all our adult lives, the two of us. Alfred watched Flora's performance with hard desperate eyes, awaiting his moment. Fauna all but crushed to the ice wall behind him. The boy would freeze to it if this went on too long.

—*do you feel your star plummeting, father? does your son's rise?*—

Hatred withered. With it the heat rushed out of me, all drive, everything that had kept me going. The man I faced was, in essence, me. I could hardly loathe him more than I already hated myself. Alfred had been a touch luckier, was all. There was no "better father."

But I could be the better man. There was still a little time for that.

'Honey.'

I limped cautiously toward the teetering scene, gnarled hands held out. Those remaining fingers didn't straighten anymore, joints embedded beneath the skin like chunks of flint. My voice quavered. Only an old man, no threat to anybody.

Nonetheless Alfred was quick to bare his yellow teeth at my approach. How could I communicate this sudden, irrational compassion in a way he'd hear? I'd fostered hatred all these years.

Fauna whimpered and his father barked something. We hadn't even shared the same language. Fauna's letters to my daughter effectively gibberish, to be read however her inflamed imagination fancied. How surreal their brief time on the beach must have been.

Flora staggering in out of the storm. Perhaps awkwardly pantomiming her need for shelter, companionship and love, her cheeks hot with humiliation. The men sitting silent and suspicious around Alfred's bountiful fire. She would have found herself pleading for things she'd imagined coming as naturally as an embrace.

Perhaps what Alfred saw approaching now loomed with the same finality in his mythos as he had in mine: a withered demon. An unstoppable force that should've been dead a thousand times over but refused to be shaken, clutching his heels no matter what he dared.

The despair that must be rending him to finally find himself trapped. Such extremities drive men to do terrible things.

Alfred began to climb. It couldn't believe it, it was superhuman. His almost-adult son dangling down his bowed back, hands cinched around his tortoise neck—could the boy even hang on that long? When I tilted my head back the ice wall ascended all the way up into a sky that wanted to blind me. It began to lurch and whirl, sweat popped out all over, and I brought my vision down quickly.

Flora glanced at me doubtfully. She touched the ice and then flinched back, hissing in deep-freeze pain even through her gloves. I dared to hope.

'Come on, baby.'

I held my ruined old hand out to her, gesturing back the way we came.

'Come on. It's over.'

Flora began hauling herself up the craggy ice face in pursuit.

I swallowed, throat a dry click, and the blue light off the glacier rang inside my head. They were making it child's play to follow: laying a path of lurid crimson smears up the ascent, as gloves and then skin tore free. That indecent red. I'd seen those colours paired before.

—*brimstone red on madonna blue. i remembered being fevered with the chase. and a little boy had been pointing. they'd given me my daughter, once, even as i'd been mad for their lives—*

It couldn't end here. I took a reluctant grip on the first handhold and strained to lift. It was torture. Flimsy T-rex arms weren't suited to this, with the muscle melted away. I didn't think I'd get off the ground.

Both whole of hand and foot, Alfred and Flora were pulling ahead. As I gained altitude every millimetre of me shook with the strain; all I wanted was to let go and die. Stop this. Just smash against the stones below.

And that awful cold. The glacier struck to the core of you, burned away what made you human. I crept up its skin in the slowest, most excruciating chase ever. And I found the glacier was not without opinions on this. From deep within the surface I ascended came slow yawing groans. Weary plates of ice that must be the staggering size of cities were sagging together, shoving, wanting relief of their own.

And ... whispers? Coming from in there. I had to hold my breath to hear, and was already gasping from my climb; still, that's what it sounded like. Somewhere between rustling and a low human murmur, conveying an urgent message I really ought to heed. A prognostication. A grim warning. If every strand of my hair weren't already struggling on double-duty to keep me warm it would've stuck out like quills.

Up another step. I groaned and hugged the ice. I dipped my forehead to rest, and came face-to-face with Mai's wide blood-veined eye peeping out at me through a hairline crack.

With a choked scream I flailed, caught my grip again. The vision vanished: just ice, blue and luminous. I must be hallucinating. Now that I had my head screwed on the crevice was far too twisting and narrow to accommodate any human form without the most unnatural compression and contortion into a spaghetti-person, threaded through the gaps. Besides, nobody could survive baking in that chill. It was rapidly becoming the end of me.

While I hung there, panting, trying to muster both sanity and bravery to continue, a flicker in the periphery caught my notice. Movement where there shouldn't be any—all the people were above me. Dread turned my muscles to water. If fingers and toeless feet hadn't been jammed in tight, I would have fallen.

I couldn't bear to see. I couldn't not look. Like clockwork driven by fatalism, I slowly turned my head.

This crack in the ice was bigger, deep, and dark. Blue became purple. Puffs of cold eddied out. I had to lean closer, to squint into its depths, which was the last thing I wanted to do.

Upside-down with his head crushed onto his shoulder, Uncle Ebo leered back at me, mouth dropped open in voiceless delight. I blinked, and he vanished, too.

No. No, Uncle Ebo didn't vanish the way a hallucination might. He pulled back. *Slithered* further back into the glacier.

Had I been cold? Suddenly I was burning up with panic. Scrabbling higher in my haste to be away. I seemed to float above the deadly drop.

Somnambulistic curses blurted out of the very gaps I had to stuff my hands into but I wouldn't listen to them, I wouldn't! The cold breath that gusted against my cheek was Ebo's. Mai eyeballed me again ...

—*peek jim!*—

... from her new lair beneath an overhang. Her eyes and mouth were gaping voids drilled into her face, wider and rounder than seemed reasonable.

She mouthed the air and whisked away when spotted; but too slowly, as though making damn sure she'd been seen. I couldn't look at anything else. I wasn't even watching where I put my feet.

'Don't look at them, Daddy!'

Flora's voice came bouncing down. She sounded … annoyed? Angry? The glacier moaned as though trying to drown her out.

'They're animals. They want you to fall.'

Animals populating the glacier? Poor squashed things inhabiting the cracks, squirming, with faces I could mistake for my lost loved ones? On them where? On their backs? Their limbs, to be dangled out like tempting bait? Worn over their own bestial features like a mask?

Or perhaps these were blank vessels, waiting like empty cysts within the ice. Ready for me to bring my own haunts and horrors to fill them up. And if I'd carried it here with me, then in a sense that could really be Mai's mocking grin, pulled tight as a leer of final agony. Pushed right up against my ear. I'd brought them here and trapped them in these … these grotesque things.

Uncle Ebo flapped his tongue at me. Mai winked, both gestures stilted and artificial. I tried so hard to see the illusion, the false face. My brain didn't agree. It wanted Mai, it wanted Uncle Ebo, the crushing addiction of love lost forever but unexpectedly found, here again, like a deadly miracle.

The beasts could be burrowing squealing into my abdomen and so long as they dangled those faces before me, even knowing the trick, I'd smile peacefully and embrace their monstrous distortions. Something had worked out that we squishy humans *needed* faces, we *wanted* faces, and we'd follow them.

I climbed. That was my job, what I had to do. Swallow the

sickness and screaming horror, and keep going.

I reached the top lip unsure if I'd have enough left to get over. Flora's knitted face didn't appear: apparently warning me about the glacier animals had cut into her busy schedule too much already. Luckily my legs were the best part of what was left of me. One big kick—which almost wasn't enough, I crashed down on my chest with lower half still dangling and kicking in space and I could feel that slide back, feel it start to happen. I roll-flopped sideways to get my legs up, that last push of momentum and it was over. I lay gasping full length on the glacier's crown. I was up.

I'd like to say they were getting away but Alfred had nothing left. He had carried his son up on his fucking back. He was crawling. Fauna kneeling slightly ahead, imploring him with hopeless gestures to come on. Utterly reduced, both of them. Look at how absolutely they still wanted life.

Flora loomed exultantly over Alfred. She had my brick in her hand.

'Honey, please. Let's just let them go. Forget them. Look—I've got some moss. We'll go somewhere better. Be happy, the two of us.'

Flora turned her face slowly toward me without moving the rest of her body at all. For a moment it was like one of those things from the ice stood there, had slithered up inside her clothes and was imitating my efforts, mocking me.

She eyed my offered, trembling fistful of moss with utter bafflement.

'This is it, Daddy. We won.'

'Please. I don't want to do all this again.'

The plea wrenched from the depths of me. Just make it stop. I can't stand it.

'Do what *again*, Daddy?'

All the dirty corners laid bare. But Flora had to come to me if my shadow, the other father, was to have any kind of chance.

'The ... the goat. It wasn't a goat, baby, you *know* it wasn't.'

'There are no more goats,' she intoned hollowly in her little girl's voice. And in the voice of the glacier. Mai peered up from a million places between my feet.

I laid myself bare.

'It happened like an accident. Only I meant it. I planned it. We were starving. *You* were starving, sweetheart, you whimpered all night. I could hear you dying.'

I hit Mai from behind. Any other way and she'd have been able to defend herself. So feeble from hunger that trying to heft the chunk of concrete was akin to lifting the skyscraper it had calved from.

Down, though; down was easy. Mass brought its own momentum. It came down like every lie she ever told. Struck square in the middle of that shining hair, her balaclava off for Flora to play with. Mai fell awkwardly forward.

'Jim!' she called in her loud voice, so full of pain and fear. 'Jim, something's got me!'

Never turning to see it was me. And calling for me, my help. My vileness convulsed me and I hit her again, and again.

I put Mai's organs in a little pile, just as I'd later do with Fluffy's. All the best, the nourishment of a mother's love, went to Flora. My stomach clotted with hair and teeth I was unable to digest. Terrible pain. With every mouthful I martyred myself to the idea I'd done this awful thing for our daughter.

Surely a good man would know *why* he did such a thing. He would never suspect the real reason to be because he was screaming with hunger. Exhausted from feeling trapped, scrabbling desperation from the moment he opened his eyes 'til he slumped into sleep. Unable to spot a way out.

And absolutely not from childish uncontrolled anger at his wife's dishonesty. The way she'd ruined everything.

Had we left Mai's remains where they lay with her hair spread across the ground, I might have understood her restless haunting. She'd have hated being alone. But we carried her with us. She saved Flora.

'It was your mother, honey. It was my *duty*, to keep up my strength until you found yours. To protect you.'

Needles of ice looked back at me through ragged eye holes.

'That's always been it, hasn't it Daddy. All for me.'

I started to relax, but she wasn't done.

'Just like the nose cream.'

Flora was turning toward me, *I had her!* But Alfred couldn't hold his water any longer.

He shoved Flora, trying to knock her off balance. I didn't need to understand the language to know he shouted, 'Run!' at his crying son. No less than me, he was willing to give all for his child.

Alfred's burst of desperation was evidently something Flora had been poised in wait for. My own story had never meant that much to her. Not in the living breathing face of her own.

Lithe and powerful she seized the front of Alfred's clothing. The brick went up and down, up and down.

Was this how it would be, then? Alfred versus Flora, and my penance to raise his child?

'Stop!'

Suddenly brave, I rushed in. Tottered.

—*see me? i'm the good man; i'm the better father*—

The brick whipped around on my blind side, my vulnerable spot Flora knew so well.

—*peek, daddy*—

A *crunch* that bloomed like a flower inside of me. A moment of wonder. And then a sickening flood of pain.

That blow, so profound it rang through my life, both forward and back. Just like a kiss. They met in the middle where I, so briefly, had existed.

I blinked. Well, a wink was what it was, let's be honest. I was sideways on the glacier's burning surface, which would only steal my precious heat.

—for fuck's sake, get up!—

I sighed heavily. I could see Alfred crawling, crawling, trying to crawl away. Perhaps I could go with him this time. I had always followed: it might be nice to finally go somewhere together.

Tragically, if the tired soldiers that were my limbs were rallying around me I couldn't feel it. Flora ducked down into my limited field of vision. She did not bother pushing the balaclava up so I could see her, my Flora, my beautiful girl.

'I worked it out, Daddy. I don't have to be anyone's good girl. Fall in love. Start a family. Save *mankind*.'

She made a sharp bark without covering her mouth.

'All I need is what it takes to stay alive. Use up everything. Until one day I'll die too, and there'll be nothing left. Like you always say: *all for me*.'

She would, too, I saw. Savagely and magnificently. Completing the work on the world that humanity started. I wanted to be proud. Instead within me there was only the most dreadful fear. I had no control over what I felt, and it would go on 'til the brick put an end to it.

—my baby—

My single eye was gradually hazing over, no matter how I struggled to hold it back. Fur softly brushed my cheek as Flora stood up. I pretended it was a caress.

A strain to refocus. I saw Flora stand motionlessly over

Alfred, staring off at the edge of the glacier. Just like her fugues of old, after the seizures. I wanted to comfort her.

I blinked, and she was crouched on his chest, brick joyously pistoning. Heavy padded clothing provided the other father with some protection. Which only made it take longer. I hadn't expected dying to be so tiresome. The cold creeping on, this was purgatory.

Young Fauna was mercifully beyond my line of sight. He didn't get far. Whatever Flora did to her betrayer I couldn't escape his hysterical shrieks. A sound so horrible I longed for the long deformed stick arms to spring up from the glacier and embrace me, drag me down. Even if it was a false Mai, a yearning illusion.

I trembled as heat left me, and I prayed with all a father had that the stained, crumpled shape that used to be Alfred had gone on ahead. That he wasn't lying here as I was, listening.

Wearing Mai's true face, Flora would soon be coming back for me. Wet noises, as she went about her work.

I closed my eye.

—if i've failed at this last, please ... please remember ...—

—... everything i did was for my flora—

ALSO BY BP GREGORY

NOVELS

Flora & Jim
The Town
Something for Everything (Automatons Book #2)
Automatons (Automatons Book #1)
Outermen

NOVELLA

Only Skin

SHORT STORY COLLECTIONS

Orotund, Collected Short Stories Volume Two
Cacophony, Collected Short Stories Volume One

Kate knows what she saw: a burned out ruin. But the evidence is gone, and nobody else believes the town was ever there.

She knows the town exists. Determined to prove it at any cost, in poking around the outback Kate risks exposing herself and her friends to the slew of horrible urban legends, reticent locals, and too many people who vanished over the years with nowhere to go.

A paroled monster, a prostitute and a policeman all see a little girl lost, but this isn't the start of a joke. An isolated, frail old man trapped in his apartment; what possible threat could he pose to the sociopaths next door?

Take time for a stroll down humanity's eerie back alleys and enjoy BP Gregory's newest short science fiction, urban fantasy and horror stories neatly packaged together in Orotund: Collected Short Stories Volume Two.

Author and avid reader BP Gregory brings monsters, machines and roaming cities, insanity, betrayal and lust! With such tales you shouldn't always feel comfortable or safe.

For sneak peeks, more stories, reviews and recommendations as she ploughs through her to-read pile visit bpgregory.com.

www.ingramcontent.com/pod-product-compliance
Lightning Source LLC
LaVergne TN
LVHW040618250326
834688LV00035B/609